of
men
and
crabs

# of men
and crabs

BY JOSUÉ DE CASTRO

TRANSLATED FROM THE PORTUGUESE

BY SUSAN HERTELENDY

NEW YORK
THE VANGUARD PRESS, INC.

Manufactured in the United States of America by H. Wolff
Book Manufacturing Company

Designer: Ernst Reichl
Standard Book Number 8149–0667–2
Library of Congress Catalogue Card Number: 75–139683

CONTENTS

V

What is the meaning of literature in a hungry world? Literature, like morals, needs to be universal. The writer must therefore place himself with the great majority—two billion hungry people—if he wants to speak to all and be read by all.

JEAN-PAUL SARTRE

Do you know that the ages will pass and mankind will by the lips of its sages proclaim that there is no crime, and consequently no sin; there is only hunger?

DOSTOIEVSKY

At every inn I was met by hunger; at every well I was met by thirst.

ANDRÉ GIDE

The belly is the foundation: bread, wine and meat are the prime essentials. Only with bread, wine and meat can we create God.

NIKOS KAZANTZAKIS

a rather generous preface

Is this book really fiction? Is it not rather a kind of diary; perhaps, in a way, an autobiography? I cannot say. All I know is that the book tells the story of one being face to face with the manifold phenomena of existence: the story of a poor boy just opening his eyes to the spectacle the world afforded him of a landscape that was no more than a narrow inlet of the sea, a narrow inlet of miseries.

The theme of the book is my childhood discovery of hunger on the marshlands in the city of Recife, where I lived among those shipwrecked in this sea of misery. It was not at the Sorbonne, or at any other seat of learning, that I came to know the anatomy of hunger. It was revealed to me spontaneously in the marshes of the Capibaribe River and the more miserable sections of the city of Recife: Afogados, Pina, Santo Amaro, and the island of Leite. *That* was my university—the muddy marshes of Recife, seething with crabs and peopled by humans fashioned of crab meat, thinking and feeling like crabs; amphibians, at home on land and in water, half-man, half-animal; fed, in their infancy, on that miry milk, crab broth. Humans who began life as foster brothers to the crab; who learned to crawl and walk with them in the mud, and who, after drinking their miry milk in childhood and wallowing in the thick broth of mud and marsh and being drenched in the crab's smell of foul earth and stagnant water, could never again fight free of this muddy carapace that made them so like the crab, their brother, his tough shell also smeared with mud.

I awoke quite early to this strange mimicry of crabs by men—men dragging along, crouching low, like the crab, for survival; still, like the crab, at the water's edge, or even walking backward as does the crab.

That is why the marshland dwellers, having known life only in this clammy marsh mud, could leave the crab cycle only with difficulty, and even then only by meeting death and thereby sinking forever into the mire.

I had the impression that the denizens of the marshes —man and crab born on the edge of the river—became more deeply embedded in the mud as they grew. It was as if the dense vegetation of the marshes, with its twisted stems, with the entanglement of its wrinkled branches, and with the dense web of its piercing roots, had seized them with the finality of an octopus, piercing

XII

their flesh and all the orifices of their bodies—their eyes, their mouths, their ears—with invisible tentacles.

And so they all remained marooned in the marshlands, caught by the tentacles with which the insatiable marshes sucked all the juice from their flesh and the spirit from their enslaved souls. The mangroves would thus, with a strange force, seize control of the life of all those people, taking possession slowly, relentlessly, completely. Those strange plants that in past geological eras had conquered all of this region—the swampy basin where Recife lies today—were now extending their domination to its inhabitants. And everything in this region became a part of the conquering marsh—man, as well as earth.

In reality, the mangroves were the first conquerors of the land. They were even, to a great extent, its creator. This vast, easily floodable plain, shaped by islands, peninsulas, marshes, and swamps, was at one time a large depression, a crescent-shaped bay rimmed with hills. Two great rivers, the Capibaribe and the Beberibe, flowed into it after climbing the wall of hills, and filled the ditch with alluvial earth torn from more distant areas and carried in by their currents. Gradually, small muddy crowns emerged from the bay created by the precipitation and deposit of these materials. And it was over these still unstable banks, in this uncertain mixture of earth and water, that the mangroves proliferated that strange plant curiously able to live in salt water on loose and constantly submerged earth. Like

XIII

animals, they desperately grasped at this piece of earth for survival by means of a clawlike root system. These dug deeply into the mire and sustained one another in resisting the force of the tide currents and the strong trade winds that tousled their green hair. The mangroves gradually intertwined their roots and arms in amorous promiscuity, and thus consolidated their existence as well as that of the loose earthy group of miry crowns on which they originated. With the alluvium accumulated in that maze of roots, the level of the earth rose progressively, and its surface expanded under the thick foliage. There remains no doubt whatever that all the land that today floats at the level of the waters, in the obstructed bay of Recife, had its origin in the mangroves.

The mangroves came with the rivers and, from the materials the rivers carried, laboriously constructed their own ground in a constant battle with the sea. They came as occupation troops and, as they reached the sea, silently and progressively, they built this vast alluvial plain cut today by numerous river inlets, and densely populated by man and crab, their cohabitants and worshipers.

It is only natural that having performed this Cyclopean task, the mangrove should today be deified by the dwellers of the region, though they are unable to explain how the plant performs this divine miracle of land creation. But even today men see miry crowns grow before their eyes and by the constructive energy of the mangrove become verdant islands seething with life. Astonished, they see little islands produced around larger ones as if emerging from their wombs through a mysterious childbearing process, miraculously midwifed by the mangrove.

I was born in the city of Recife, which, with its accumulated misery, is in certain ways the Hong Kong of America, set within this group of islands floating in a slumber between the branches of the two rivers, Capibaribe and Beberibe.

The first society with which I became acquainted was the society of crabs. After that, I met the men who inhabited the marshes, foster brothers to the crab. Only much later did I come to know the other society of men—the great society. Candor compels me to say, that as I learned about life in observing these different societies, I reserve to this day the largest portion of my affection for the society of the marshes—the society of crabs and men.

It is the story of the society of these amphibians that I tell in this book; of this society that economically is also ambivalent as it vegetates on the borderlines of two economic structures that history has as yet not been able to weave into one fabric: the feudal agrarian and the capitalist. These structures persist side by side today without merging, without integrating themselves into a homogeneous type of civilization.

The society of the marshlands is a society squeezed between these two crushing structures. Compressed by them, it flows as a social mud into the vat of the marshes of Recife, blending with the viscous mud of the swamps.

I was born on a street named for the illustrious Joaquim Nabuco, great slave abolitionist of the time of the Empire:

"Nasci também nesta terra	I too, was born in this land
Que o sol castiga e descora	Beaten and bleached
	by the sun
—Terra de Joaquim Nabuco—	Land of Joaquim Nabuco—
Homem de bem, homem certo	A man who was
	righteous and just
Que era muito diferente	Very different, you understand
Désses 'Nabucos' de agora."	From the "Nabucos" of today.

(Joaquim Cardoso, *O Coronel de Macambira,* 1963)

The house where I was born had next to it a large fishpond with fish, crabs, and other similar crustaceans. If I was not born inside the fishpond with the crabs, at two I was already in it. One day I slipped in the mud of its banks and was removed from its waters half-drowned. Thereafter, diving into the waters of the marsh became a habit. I then moved to Madalena, a neighborhood closer to the river, into an old colonial house only one story high, with six large front windows. It was a large house, and it seemed crushed by the weight of its own structure. It was set like a fortress on high ramparts through which, at high tide, the crabs would climb to the terrace, some of them even daring to enter the rooms. The house would then become a Noah's ark, and the whole farm would become a sea.

When the waters receded, a black mud remained, covering the landscape for days. The house faced the river because it was built in the old days when all transportation from the city was by boat and barge. The businessmen of the sugar trade would go to their offices in their black frock coats and top hats, rowed by bare-torsoed Negroes up the Capibaribe.

Our small farm had many animals and trees—mango trees and sapodillas, that bore delicious fruits. Delicious also were the fruits of other trees not found on our farm but which would appear strewn on the ground. These were fruits picked during the night in the neighborhood gardens by bats, which dropped them in their hurried flights: guavas, *jambos* and *araçás,* all half-chewed, but which delighted me during my morning walks in the garden, sponging on the nocturnal labors of the bats, my circumstantial associates. On the farm were also cows, horses, sheep, and goats, all of which, during high tide, would crowd up on the terrace. Birds of all kinds sang in the large cages that hung all over the place. My father had brought to Recife the entire living landscape of his home, its animals and its birds. In the garden, I breathed this landscape transplanted from those remote and arid plains. And from the front of the house I contemplated another landscape: the dark landscape of the marsh.

Right next to the house started the tightly packed zone of the hovels—straw and mud huts, piled one on top of the other in a network of alleys in desperate anarchy. The houses penetrated the water, the tide invaded them. The branches of the river overtook the street and the mire overwhelmed everything.

I was brought up in the miry marshes of the Capibaribe, whose waters, as they flowed before my avid young eyes, seemed perpetually to be telling a story. They told me the story of their long adventures as they descended to the different regions of the northeast; the gray backlands where my father was born and from which he emigrated with his entire family during the drought of '77, and the green lands of the cane plantations in the fertile northeastern zone of the *Zona da Mata,* where my mother, the daughter of a sugar plantation owner, was born.

This was the story the river whispered to me in its sweet language as it timorously passed through the green-gray backlands: voluminous when it flowed through the sea of the unending cane plantations, and peaceful through the miry sea of marshes, till it fell into the bosom of the sea itself. For hours I would sit motionless at the quay, listening to the story of the river, watching its waters flow as if it were a motion picture.

It was the river that first taught me the history of the northeast, the history of this land that almost lacks a history. The truth of the matter is that the story of the man of the northeast reached me more through the eyes than the ears. It entered my eager, young eyes in the shape of images that were not always clear and cheerful.

XVIII

It was with these somber images of the marshes and mud that I started creating the world of my childhood. I saw nothing that did not instill in me a sense of real discovery. That was how I saw and felt tingling in me the terrible discovery of hunger. I discovered the hunger of an entire population enslaved by the anguish of looking for something to eat. I saw the crabs seething with hunger at the edge of the water, in wait for the current to bring them food—a dead fish, a fruit peel, or a piece of dung that they would drag to a dry spot and, with it, satisfy their hunger. I also saw men seated on the railing of the old quay murmuring monosyllables, a stalk of grass between their lips from which they drew its green juice, while from the corners of their mouths ran a greenish saliva that seemed to me to have the same origin as the foam of the crab: it was the dribble of hunger. Little by little, because of its obsessive presence, this vague specter of hunger revealed itself to me and gained shape and meaning in my spirit. I slowly came to understand that the entire life of these people forever centered around one simple obsession: the anguish of hunger. Their very speech referred to nothing else. Their slang was heavy with words that evoked food, those foods they desired with uncontrollable appetite. They might be referring to anything at all when they said "it's a soup," for they meant "it's a cinch"; "it's fish roe" meant "like hell!"; they said "it's a pineapple" for "it's a dud"; or "bread-bread, cheese-cheese" for "frankly." It was as if this slang were a kind of

mental compensation for being perpetually famished—
an entire population with an empty stomach and a
head full of imagined foods. Food had gone to their
heads as sex goes to the heads of those who starve for
love.

The constant presence of hunger was at all times the
major force that shaped the moral behavior of the men
in this community, their ethical values, their hopes, and
their most powerful feelings. To see them act, speak,
fight, suffer, live, and die was to see hunger itself with
its despotic iron hands shaping the heroes of mankind's
greatest drama, the drama of hunger. This was what
my frightened young eyes saw without quite understanding the drama's tragic meaning. I thought at first
that hunger was a sad privilege of the marshland region
where I lived. I later discovered that in the northeastern
geography of hunger, the marshlands were a real Promised Land that attracted men from other areas in which
hunger was even greater. They came from the region
of droughts and from the zone where nothing was
grown but sugar cane, an industry that, with lofty indifference, crushed man and cane, reducing everything
to bagasse.

I took an entire course on hunger just by listening
with ever-growing interest to the interminable stories
my father told about the bitter hardships suffered by
our family in the drought of 1877. I learned in more
detail about the presence of hunger in the sugar zone
through the monotonous tales of two old Negroes who

had been slaves in their youth, and who retrieved their memories of that time as they cut hay for my father's horses.

Even when I sought distraction in watching the market singers or the presentation of the *Bumba-meu-boi*, a popular and traditional pageant presented in the region of the hovels, what I saw before me acting, speaking, gesticulating, was hunger in its many guises. Guitar players sang:

"Triste a vida de posseiro　　A settler's life is harsh
junto a Alagoa Amarela　　There at Yellow Marsh
Vinte anos sôbre a terra　　Twenty years on the land
cavando o faltoso pão,　　Digging for scanty bread
vinte anos de promessa　　Twenty years of promises
com a mesma enxada na mão,　　With the same hoe in my hand
catorze filhos no mundo　　Fourteen children in the world
fora os que estão no caixão."　　Besides the ones who are dead.

"Peguei na espingarda velha　　The way I'd grip my hoe
como quem pega o enxadão　　I gripped my rifle instead
com a fôrça que　　With the strength that hunger
　a fome dá　　gives
pra quem defende　　To those who defend their
　seu pão."　　bread.

(Alfonso Romano de Sant' Ana,
Morte na Alagoa Amarela.)

In the *Bumba-meu-boi* I saw a strange two-footed ox, the most human ox I had encountered in my short life, suffering like a man, crying and rebelling as men do. And I fell in love with that thin, dry ox, so thin and so dry that truthfully it was only a head with horns, gigantic horns that swayed in the air as if the ox were only a specter. In fact, the ox was all horns and skin; it had no flesh. As told by the herdsman in his song, when he felt the ox all over, he never found a sign of flesh:

"*Eu fui ver na cabeça*   I took a look at his head
Eh! Bumba!
Achei ela bem lefa   And found it quite sad.
Eh! Bumba!

Eu fui lá na ponta   I took a look at his horn
Eh! Bumba!
Ela de mim não fez conta   It left me untorn.
Eh! Bumba!

Eu fui ver no pescoço   I took a look at his neck
Eh! Bumba!
Achei êle bem torto   It was nothing but a wreck.
Eh! Bumba!

Eu fui ver nas apá   I took a look at his leg
Eh! Bumba!
Não achei nada lá   It was bony like a peg.
Eh! Bumba!

Eu fui ver lá na mão   I took a look at his hand
Eh! Bumba!
Não achei nada não   I couldn't understand.
Eh! Bumba!

Eu fui ver nas costelas   I took a look at his rib
Eh! Bumba!
Não achei nada nelas   It was open like a crib.
Eh! Bumba!"

XXII

"Eu fui ver no vazio	I took a look at the air
Eh! Bumba!	
Achei o boi bem esguio	I saw the ox shining there.
Eh! Bumba!	
Eu fui ver no chambari	I took a look at his feet
Eh! Bumba!	
Não achei nada ali	There wasn't any meat.
Eh! Bumba!	
Eu fui ver no cocotó	I took a look at his knuckle
Eh! Bumba!	
Andei bem ao redor	It was scratchy like a buckle.
Eh! Bumba!	
Eu fui ver na rabada	I took a look at his tail
Eh! Bumba!	
Não achei ali nada	It was smaller than a nail.
Eh! Bumba!"	

The *Bumba-meu-boi* was no more than the nightmare of the famished; the famished dreaming of the phantom of an ox that grows before their greedy eyes but whose meat disappears under their searching hands.

And so, through the stories of the men and the route of the river, I learned that hunger was not an exclusive product of the marshlands; that the marshlands only attracted the famished northeasterners, those from the region of droughts and those from the region of sugar cane. They were all attracted to this Promised Land and snuggled in that nest of mud built by the two rivers where there was the wonderful cycle of the crab. I grew up and wandered into the world and, as I came upon

XXIII

new landscapes, I noticed with renewed surprise that what I had imagined to be a local occurrence was a universal drama; that the human scene of the marsh was to be found all over the world; that the characters of Recife's mire were identical to those of numerous hunger-ravaged areas of the world; that the human mire of Recife, which I had known in my childhood, still soils the vista of our planet with dark blots of misery —the dark demographic patches in the geography of hunger.

However, I have already shown this in other essays I have written on hunger, essays of a scientific nature or offering a sociological analysis of the problem. What I have not told before was my own encounter with the specter of hunger. Today I decided to tell of it; to tell not only of the encounter itself, but of the fear it engendered in me. I met the monster in the marshlands of the Capibaribe, and never again was I able to escape from its tragic fascination. It is this fascination and this scar left by hunger in my soul as a child that I am trying to evoke in this story about men and crabs.

Some of the things I tell in this book have disappeared, but others—most of them—remain as I saw them when I was a child. This is so because time means little in the lands of misery, in the underdeveloped lands of the third world where hunger and death, with their perpetual presence, are forever shaping the fate of man.

J. C.

XXIV

*of
men
and
crabs*

I

of how the body and soul of João Paulo became imbued with crab broth . . .

Recife, city of rivers, bridges, and old mansions, is also the city of *mocambos:* huts, shacks of clay rough-cast by hand, and roofed with straw, coconut palm, or tin-plate.

In the cold June dawn, at the time when the darkness of night still lingers but a morning breeze is beginning to stir, the marshlands were sleeping quietly, sunk in the peaceful mud. The only sound, from time to time, was a cricket singing in the hovels and a frog answering out in the dark night. Along the Motocolombó road, which was almost invisible in the midst of the marshlands at this hazy hour, came the first peasants with their baskets of fruits and vegetables, rushing to set up their stalls in the Afogados market before day-light. The road, hollowed out by the May rains, was nothing but mud, and the flat feet of the peasants sank

27

deep into the soft earth, the mud oozing through their toes as they moved on, bent under the weight of their baskets.

The morning also moved on, making its way through the mist of the quagmire. Then, suddenly, the milky air condensed and a cold rain pelted the ground as if it were an enormous drum. A violent streak of lightning revealed the entire flooded plain and gave luster to the large mangrove leaves that swayed in the strong wind. The rumble of the thunderclaps drowned out the songs of the crickets and frogs.

The peasants, frightened by the storm, hurriedly reached into their baskets and took out the burlap sacks that they kept wrapped around their wooden clogs and improvised some hoods to protect them from the rain. And so, resembling the ghosts of medieval monks with these grotesque burlap hoods, the peasants pressed forward. The rugged road was now crossed in every direction by crabs that, roused from sleep by the storm, ran in terror from the thunderclaps and occasionally were crushed under the feet of the peasants with the dry crack of breaking twigs.

The rain stopped, the sun came out, and into the light of day emerged this eerie landscape of marshes—an uneven amalgam of earth and water inhabited by strange amphibians—the men and the crabs who live in the marshlands of the river Capibaribe.

The marshlands of Recife are a paradise for the crab. If the earth and everything on it was created for man, then the marshes were especially created for the crab. There, everything is, was, or will become crab, including the mud and the man who lives in it—the mud mixed with urine, excrement, and other residues brought by the tide. What is not yet crab shall become crab, that mire-born creature that lives from mire, fattens on its filth and out of it produces the white meat of its legs and the greenish jelly of its slimy entrails.

On the other hand, the people live by catching crabs, sucking their legs, eating and licking their shells until they are clean as glass; and from that mire comes flesh. There are two hundred thousand individuals, two hundred thousand citizens made of crab meat. Whatever the system rejects returns as debris to the mire of the marshlands, once again to become crab.

In the apparent serenity of the quagmire the tragic and silent cycle of the crab unfolds: the cycle of hunger that devours both man and crab as each struggles in the mire.

Across this murky landscape, which was now vibrating under the harsh light of the tropics reflected in the large mirrors of the tidewaters, shrill and insistent cries resounded. They were factory whistles impatiently calling people to work, people who live in the poor sections of Afogados, Santo Amaro, and the island of Leite. The still-dozing people of the hovels were awakened by the whistles. Some were sharp and violent; others were deeper and more drawn out. The neighborhood of the hovels began to swarm with life, as if it were the marsh itself boiling over with crabs. Through the cracks in the roofs and the gaps in the doors a strong smell of smoke and coffee escaped; then came the insistent clatter of coughing and bawling children. The people of the hovels were showing signs of life and preparing themselves to live a new day in the crab cycle.

The hovel doors opened and the marsh dwellers began to appear in the alleys with worn, sleepy faces. The men were rushing, their lunchboxes under their arms; the women moved more slowly, lifting their skirts as they looked for drier places to step, carefully jumping over the muddy puddles with a certain horror of cold water. The children were up too, plunging into the marshes, the younger ones naked and the older ones with a rag covering their sex. But all dove into the mud to catch crabs with pleasure and without second thought, their naked bodies indifferent to the cold of the water and the pricking of mosquitoes that buzz hungrily among the thick leaves of the mangroves.

João Paulo was awakened by the factory whistles. His eyes still shut, the boy sat up sleepily on his straw bed. He clumsily rubbed his face and, still half asleep, opened his eyes, stretched and yawned. Then, looking around, his eyes fell on his two younger brothers sleeping in another corner of the cubicle and his parents sitting at the table eating breakfast. He stretched his hand toward them and said sleepily:

"Your blessing, Father, your blessing, Mother."

"God bless you, my son," they answered.

João Paulo leaped from his bed and opened the back door of the hovel. The sun hit his thin, dark face with its prominent cheekbones. Enraptured, his deep dark eyes contemplated the tide as it rose to the door of the hovel. The sun hemmed the miry stains of the mangroves with a silvery fringe made of small luminous patches. João Paulo went into the water and with his steps wiped out the bright and undulant fringes. He stopped as the water hit his ankles and he urinated into it. The jet of urine gleamed in the sun as if it were a rainbow and hit the water with the noise of a waterfall that seemed to fill the silence in the quagmire. This loud noise of urine hitting the water filled João Paulo with an overwhelming satisfaction. He felt like a man because he could make as much noise as the crab fishermen do when they urinate in the swamp.

With an expression of contentment, João Paulo moved on, stopped, washed his face in the murky water of the tide, and scraped the crust from his eyes. He noisily gargled with a little water to wash his mouth and then fiercely expelled it, pressing his cheeks with both hands. The water squirted out, finally falling at a great distance. He laughed, pleased with his prowess, a knack of launching water as far as gardeners do with their hoses in the gardens of the city. João Paulo dreamed about how nice it would be to someday be the gardener in a rich house of this city, the outlines of which, with its tall buildings, he could see in the distance, while the sun dried his wet face.

How fine it would be to live always with the good odor of garden plants, and to lightly tread green, soft grasses instead of constantly smelling the stench of the tide and perpetually having to walk in the mire as if one were a crab!

His father's voice calling from the house roused João Paulo from his dream. He kicked the water hard, splashing it all over, and then went into the hovel to eat.

He sat at the table with his parents and started to drink the crab broth cooked in water and salt, and to suck the shells and the legs of the crustaceans. His two younger brothers still slept curled and wrapped in a patchwork quilt while their parents ate in silence. His mouth filled with the white crabmeat, João Paulo asked:

"Father, why did we come to live here in the marshlands?"

"Because when we came from the country, it was here that we found our Promised Land, our paradise," answered Zé Luis calmly.

"Paradise for the crabs," added João Paulo's mother in a tone of revolt.

But the boy returned to his question:

"But why here, in the marshlands? Why didn't we go

32

to the city, to the other side of the marshlands? It is so beautiful there, so different—like another world."

"It was fate, João Paulo, that brought us here," answered the father.

"The other side is the paradise of the rich; this is the paradise of the poor," said his mother, looking him straight in the eye.

But the boy's eyes opened just a little wider and retained that same puzzled look that means he cannot understand why his family has chosen such a sad and ugly place to live when there are so many beautiful places in the world; why they have chosen to live in the dark mire of the marshlands.

The sound of the Afogados church bell calling the faithful to mass came through the door of the hovel. Reminded of the time, Zé Luis hurried João Paulo along:

"Son, one of these days I'll tell you why we came here to live. There is no time today. The six-o'clock mass is about to start and in a little while the pastor will want to go crabbing and he will be impatient if you keep him waiting. Finish your food fast and run over to the house of Father Aristides. Take these crabs to please him and don't linger on the way or you'll be late."

II

of how
João Paulo saw
the knights of misery
in their strange
mud armor . . .

Whistling softly, João Paulo set out for the priest's house, one hand in his pocket and the other swinging a bundle of crabs tied together with a piece of string that he twirled from time to time.

This was the first time João Paulo was bringing a gift to Father Aristides, and he was a little worried about how the priest would receive it—this present his father had advised him to take the priest to please him.

As he walked through the marshland, the familiar scenes of the neighborhood soon made him forget his worries. A few steps away from his hovel he met the Negress Idalina squatting in the doorway of her hut and warming herself in the sun. João Paulo asked after her grandchild, Oscarlindo, who had been his constant companion at catching crabs before João Paulo got his job at the priest's house. The Negress smiled, showing her toothless gums:

"Carlindo left early to get Baé's food. Baé is already growling with hunger. Listen to his screeches."

It was true. From the back of the hut came the repeated and urgent grunts of a pig Idalina was raising in the hope of fattening him with the garbage leftovers of the rich houses and selling him at Christmas for a good price. She had bought the pig when he was quite small and kept him tied to a little shed at the edge of the marshes, where he did nothing but demand food all day.

"I've never seen such gluttony in my life. This creature whines, kicks, and scatters mud all day long asking for more food. But it's a pleasure to see how he has developed. He's like a ball of fat."

Now that Baé was fat and worth plenty of money, Idalina worried that a thief would come and take him during the night. That would be stealing her hopes of selling the pig at the Afogados market at the approaching fiestas, and getting the money to buy Carlindo a suit and a pair of shoes for his first communion.

Every night the Negress wanted to bring the pig into the house, but she restrained herself, knowing that no one could sleep with the uproar he would create snoring and grubbing all over the hovel. So she resigned herself to leaving him outside, but slept with her ears pricked and alert to the slightest suspicious sound, and only one eye closed. Her other eye was always open, watching the pig and seeing his fat image, his round body, his grizzled muzzle, and his small malicious eyes set in thick bags of fat.

Idalina's sleep was an eternal dream of love between herself and the pig. But it was also a dream filled with nightmares. One night, a hungry dog, attracted by the smell of garbage, started a quarrel with the pig over the scraps of food. The pig got furious and made a terrible racket. Idalina thought that this time it was really a thief. She got up with a start and ran to the yard, broom in hand to rescue the pig from the clutches of the bastard, only to find, to her relief, a skinny dog fleeing with his tail between his legs.

Now Idalina invited João Paulo to take a look at her treasure, her precious pig. While the two peeked through the enclosure at the fat and filthy ball growling and rolling over in the foul mire, the Negress told the youngster, in a voice filled with tenderness, that all that fat and lard forming deep pleats in the pig's skin were exclusive products of Carlindo's daily work.

Her grandson left every morning with a kerosene can, and from the garbage of the rich homes collected food remains to feed her pig. He had to leave very early, before the sun rose, to arrive there before the garbage truck. He wasted a lot of time emptying cans to remove discarded rice, chicken bones, pieces of hard bread, rotten fruits, legumes, and vegetables. It was a bitter task performed under the constant threat of being caught in the act by the watchman or the gardener of the rich houses, who would then start chasing him with screams of "Rascal! Garbage thief! Messing up the sidewalk!"

There had been several occasions when Oscarlindo was forced to abandon his debris, can and all, and dash down the street, terrified at the thought of being beaten and ending up at the police station.

On such unfortunate days, when the boy returned empty-handed, the hovel would become hell. Idalina would fall into tears of pity for her little pig that had nothing to eat, and the latter in turn would howl like a boar, scaring the entire neighborhood with his shrieks and grunts.

But there were great days, too, as for instance that memorable one when Oscarlindo found in one single house three enormous garbage cans crammed with food—remains of a wedding banquet that had taken place the evening before—and for which he required three trips to carry home all that wealth. The feast was a general one. The day of the banquet the pig ate so much he slept all afternoon without grunting once. And Idalina herself used leftover garbage—fruits still quite edible for her and her grandson.

It is a pity that weddings were not more frequent! Frequent were the banquets at the important politicians' houses. Oscarlindo knew this, but he also knew that at their entrances there were always guards who let no one touch anything, not even the garbage.

After having complimented Baé for her beauty and

fat, João Paulo went on his way, a little sad for not having seen his friend Oscarlindo.

As he reached the end of the alley that winds up at the river edge, a strong beam of light hit his eyes and João Paulo's face brightened in a broad smile, like a flower that opens under the sun's gentle touch. That beam of light was a morning message of greetings sent him by his big friend Cosme, who lived in his hovel set far in the depth of the thicket.

Turning quickly toward Cosme's hovel, João Paulo saw in the distance, over the ledge of the low window, a piece of mirror sparkling in the sun. That was all he saw, but he knew that this mirror was held in the expert hand of Cosme, the paralytic, and that the mirror at that moment was collecting João Paulo's image, his good morning, and his fraternal greeting. Hurriedly taking his hand out of his pocket, João Paulo made a large gesture saluting his friend who, stretched as usual on his bed, reflected the pageant of life in his tiny hand-mirror.

João Paulo felt like changing his itinerary and stopping at Cosme's house for a chat. But he remembered he was in a hurry to get to the priest's house. He remembered his father's injunction to be on time, and he also feared being scolded by the pastor. So he repeated with his hand the sweeping, cordial gesture and proceeded on his way.

At night, before going to bed, he would visit his friend. He would listen to the beautiful stories Cosme would tell about the large world he traveled, and the extraordinary adventures he had when his feet still served him. Today only his arms obeyed him; the legs were finished. They were dry spindlelegs, with only skin and bones and no flesh at all. He could not even move them—they were dead; they had died in the Amazon.

Eighteen years ago, long before João Paulo was born, Cosme became paralyzed in both legs. He became bedridden and never got up again. Isolated from the world, tossed like a shred of rag into his hovel, Cosme's only diversion is the small hand-mirror through which he communicated with the world. As he lay with his head next to the low window of his hut, Cosme directed the light of his mirror toward the road, which has a crossing at the distant river edge, right where João Paulo was passing now, and in that piece of glass Cosme always captured a glimpse of life. And in that way he nourished his own ragged life. That little hand-mirror was his entire world, the limited world of his senses.

The dark muddy road wound alongside the river, its banks covered by mangroves with their twisted roots, and various living tableaus turned up, one after the other, delighting João Paulo, who was always enraptured by the panorama of the world. The line of hovels extended uninterruptedly by the water's edge. At the door of one of them stood two completely naked boys, their swollen bellies projecting as if they were two drums stuck on legs that were more like thin, twisted twigs, gray with dry mud. João Paulo flicked his fingers twice on the tense bellies of the two boys, repeating in a playful tone, "Tin-tin belly," and his gesture produced a hollow sound, as hollow as if he were really striking a drum—tin-tin. . . .

On the edge of the city where brick and tile houses began to appear, João Paulo ran into a gang of boys playing soccer with a ball made of a lady's stocking stuffed with rags. They played with enormous enthusiasm, executing incredible pirouettes with the ball. João Paulo stopped for a moment, compelled by a tremendous urge to participate in the game and stay all day playing there in the street with those boys. But he remembered his duty, and his father's admonition that he be on time at the pastor's house. So he decided to continue on his way. At the exact moment he was leaving, the ball accidentally came his way and, contrary to anyone's expectations, João Paulo kicked it with such violence that it crossed the small field in the air and fell into the water, getting lost under the mangroves. The outraged gang insulted him and approached him aggressively for a revengeful settling of accounts. João Paulo made off in a rush with the bundle of crabs swaying in the air and a mocking smile on his face, happy at his revenge against these idle ones who did not have to work on such a beautiful day, with the sun shining as if it were a painting.

Tired of running, João Paulo stopped farther ahead to catch his breath, and from the edge of the quagmire he contemplated the tranquil landscape. He squatted by the water and looked close at the motionless crabs foaming in the sun as if they were a herd of oxen ruminating in a field. Scenes from his early years came to his mind: images of the yard on the farm where he was born, the barren yard where the hot sun of the backlands burned on the gleaming stones, and where the motionless oxen ruminated in silence as a whitish and slimy dribble ran slowly from their mouths—a dribble resembling the foam of the crabs.

The memories clashed and got mixed up in his mind. There were things João Paulo remembered as well as if he were seeing them happening right then, as he contemplated the crabs foaming at the edge of the water. But there were other memories that were a little vague, even mixed up, and seemed to have happened to someone other than himself. It was because João Paulo sometimes saw himself as if he were another boy—a boy whose childhood adventures he knew through the tales of his mother. The adventures of João Paulo of the backlands were a little different from the ones of João Paulo of the city.

The memory was so strong, the boy could almost smell the corral that stood next to his house in the backlands. The acrid smell of the ruminating cows, the sour smell of spilled milk, the sharp smell of cattle dung— all these smells blended together to bring to mind a vivid scene from his early childhood. From his room, he could hear the noises of the corral—his father and the cowhands made the cattle rise to their feet and then they milked them. The calves bellowed in despair, impatiently demanding their mothers' teats. These were the noises that woke him each morning. He would stand on his bed and lean on the window that opened on the corral. His father would then bring him a mug of warm milk, covered with a large ring of white foam, which he drank with relish. He remembered clearly that his upper lip was always graced by a foamy mustache that his father would clean with a rough finger as he repeated his usual phrase, "You're a man now, even a mustache you have." João Paulo would smile in contentment and remain watching the young calves as they hit the cows' udders so that the milk would descend faster to the teats.

One day João Paulo woke up much earlier than usual. He had gone to sleep without his dinner and woke with a burning stomach that impatiently demanded the sweet warmth of the customary morning milk. He opened the wooden window. The sun had not yet appeared and no one was in the corral other than the cows and their calves awaiting the cowhands. Suddenly João Paulo felt an urgent desire to suck, like a calf, at the teat of one of the cows, a desire to suck its breasts and rub his face against the cow's udder. He quickly jumped out of the window and went toward Malhada, who seemed more impatient than the others or was, perhaps, more affectionate toward her son, for she mooed standing next to the gate of the corral. He crouched under the cow's belly and with the pleasure of someone committing a sin, he started to draw on the teats. There was no milk in them. They were soft and limp—not swollen as they are when milk descends from them. So, imitating the calves, João Paulo struck the cow's udder with his head. Malhada, however, did not like the idea, and with a smart kick knocked him to the ground. João Paulo's face fell right into the heap of dung in the corral. At that exact moment, Zé Luis arrived and understood everything at once. He helped his son up and looked at that face sticky with mud and dung, the shirt covered with dust. He smiled and said, "Now you're a real calf, covered with spit and shit; and also a thief-calf, one of those who secretly suck all their mother's milk." And then Zé Luis hit João Paulo lightly on his buttocks with the same gentleness with which he hit the thin rumps of the disobedient calves.

The loud noise of a low-flying airplane broke João Paulo's train of thought, his memories of the remote countryside. The sound of the motors increased with a tremendous vibration and the plane passed like a meteor over the boy's head. The sound diminished until it was completely gone. With his eyes, João Paulo followed the plane in its flight until it disappeared over the horizon. Again he returned to the crabs, which were moving uneasily, probably frightened by the infernal sound of the plane.

It was as if the vibration of the motors had suddenly

44

broken the crystal of his abstraction in which the boy saw reflected, with incredible clarity, the images within his own being as it became conscious of the world. Disappointed, as if a sudden wave of sadness had overwhelmed his soul, João Paulo breathed deeply. And the air he breathed now was no longer that air filled with the warm and exciting smells of the backlands—the smell of perspiring cattle, the smell of still-hot manure, and the smell of live, pregnant earth. What he now smelled was the cold odor of rotten mire, of dead and decaying earth, an odor of earth carrion that must excite the smell and appetite of vultures and famished dogs, but that left João Paulo numb, almost nauseated.

Reacting against this depression, a great yearning for freedom was ignited in João Paulo's young soul, an urge to fly from that still and monotonous human landscape, to leave everything, to break with the close circle of his family, to break with the crab cycle, with the whole city of Recife. It was a desperate desire to free himself from the chains that tied him to the sticky mire of the valley of the Capibaribe and its slimy mangroves. João Paulo felt like traveling aimlessly through the world, like the ships that passed along the shore letting out with indifference an arrogant ribbon of smoke from their long, thick stacks which, to the eyes of the boy, seemed to be the unmistakable sign of their sex: male ships of indisputable courage.

To this precocious boy, in whom puberty was already swelling the flesh as well as the mind, a real man always had to be like that, like a ship on the high seas never entering a pier. It should only graze the edges of docks to enjoy sweet contact with the earth, and then go into the world in search of new smells, new contacts with other lands. The more the tide rose and the silvery fringe of foam covered the mire, the more João Paulo's despair grew and the more he wished to break with the enveloping marshlands. His muscles contracted, as if to free themselves from this coercion that smothered his body and soul. He felt that the mangroves had caught him unprepared in that position—crouched at the edge of the water—and were taking advantage of it in order to enclose him in a web woven by their thinnest roots and their most twisted branches.

To free himself from the meshes of this invisible net, João Paulo suddenly leaped up from the edge of the marsh and, on his feet now, he perceived at a distance a group of crab fishermen up to their thighs in mud, advancing in the marshland mire. They were three dark young men covered entirely with a thick miry husk resembling a suit of armor. To the eyes of João Paulo, these human creatures seemed to be the heroes of the old knightly tales that Cosme had told him. They were like giants, their bodies built of big blocks of mud, quarried from the marsh itself, shaped right there, as the crabs were created from the fermentation of the quagmire. For João Paulo, these men, knights of poverty with their armor of mire, and the crabs with their hard shells, were the heroes of a world apart. They were members of the same family, of the same nation, and the same class: the hero clan of the marshlands. And João Paulo felt himself a member of that family. He unconsciously identified with these creatures; he felt fraternally bound to man and crab, conquerors of the marshes.

As they approached the edge of the quagmire, where the ground seethed with crabs, the fishermen lay down and, sinking their arms into the mire, started to catch crabs. João Paulo, watching this exciting scene, forgot his obligations for the moment and attentively followed the precise movements and keen dialogue of the fishermen. Crawling on the ground, their stomachs and thighs against the mud, the oldest of the fishermen said to the youngest one who was still somewhat inexperienced:

"Rub more mud on your body, José, otherwise the mosquitoes will eat you alive." And José answered:

"I've already rubbed a lot, but the mosquitoes are dead hungry today; they are biting, pricking even through the mud. But I don't pay attention to mosquitoes. They can bite as much as they want. I am used to it. They don't take a piece off you, they just make you itch; and even scratching is nice."

Saying this, José twisted his body with delight and scratched his buttocks and his naked back with his muddy hands. João Paulo laughed at these conversations among the fishermen and, suddenly remembering his obligations, dashed off to the house of the parish priest that stood on a little square right next to the church.

The mass ended as he reached the square. Poor women with black scarfs on their heads came down the steps of the church and scattered along the edges of the square. The priest, heavy, with short arms, a round face, and fat, healthy cheeks, appeared at the main entrance of the church. João Paulo approached, kissed his hand with respect, and with a shy gesture offered him the crabs he had brought as a gift. The priest smiled, thanked João Paulo, and told him to give them to old Ana, his cook. Then, placing his hand on the boy's head, he took him to his house.

The sacristan had already closed the doors of the church when a wizened, thin little man, with the scared look of country people, appeared on the square and advanced hurriedly. The man wore a large leather hat on his head and carried a live turkey under his arm. Seeing the front doors of the church closed, he impatiently searched for another entrance through which he could get to the temple and speak to the priest. At that moment the priest reappeared at the door of his house, accompanied by João Paulo. The man's hopes were renewed and he rushed toward the priest. But, still a little distance away, he stopped and hesitated. The figure of the priest puzzled him. Father Aristides appeared carrying an enormous drum in one hand and a large straw basket in the other. The man had never seen a priest with a drum. A soldier walks with a drum, but priests do not. The priest smiled at the man, and his friendly smile dissipated all doubts. He really was a priest. The man approached the priest and said humbly:

"Father, I am here to fulfill a promise. I brought this turkey for the martyr Saint Sebastian." To which the priest swiftly answered:

"You are speaking to him, brother."

Again the man was perplexed; he stood motionless, making no gesture. Then the priest moved forward a step and, taking the promised turkey from the man's hands, repeated the puzzling phrase:

"You are speaking to him, brother."

III

*of Father Aristides'
strange methods for
creating storms
in order to capture
guaiamu crabs, the
tools employed, and the
consequences incurred . . .*

The dwellers of Afogados were now used to Father
Aristides' unusual methods for catching *guaiamus* and
so they were no longer frightened when, passing the
higher lands on the banks of the river, they ran across
the priest furiously striking a large drum and howling
like a wild beast.

Several months before, when the priest, accompanied
by João Paulo, first started these noisy excursions
throughout the fields, everybody was terrified. It
seemed that the priest had gone out of his mind. Everyone was sorry for him. For such a good priest, one so
dedicated to his sacerdotal duties, to suddenly lose his
mind and go off to the fields drumming furiously as if

to summon to war a host of invisible soldiers, was a heartbreaking fact. So, throughout the neighborhood, the news spread that some evil spirit had taken possession of the holy soul of the priest. He must surely be possessed by the devil.

On these occasions, the temptations of Saint Anthony became the main subject of conversation among the pious old ladies of Father Aristides' parish. Some of the faithful, more worried or more curious, came to see what was happening with their own eyes. They carefully climbed the banks of the river and, upon perceiving in the distance the massive figure of the priest with his acolyte, João Paulo, assisting in this strange ceremony which seemed like some unknown form of black magic, they would suddenly stop, perplexed, and with great care try to watch and not be seen by the priest. And the spectacle they watched was really fantastic and baffling.

Father Aristides would stop at certain mysterious points, probably indicated by some hidden sign, and then he would begin his bizarre performance: he would strike the drum and, when the resulting sounds reached their peak and reverberated terrifyingly through space, he seemed to grow as he stood on tiptoe and emitted long whistles that sounded like the wind blowing furiously across the barren plains. When the priest ended his noisy rite, João Paulo's rôle was to take his watering can and pour a long jet of water around him. It was really quite a sight. The spectators of these weird scenes fled so as not to be seen by the priest, and return to their homes in low spirits because of this inexplicable misfortune of Father Aristides.

The legend of this strange madness was spreading and had by then even reached the ears of the Archbishop of Recife. The Sacristan Veremundo, who for years had been with the church of Afogados, noticed the increase of these irrational rumors and decided to discuss them with the priest. Veremundo told him the whole story of his incomprehensible behavior that was circulating throughout the parish. He also repeated to the priest the gossip of those apparently satanic ceremonies performed in broad daylight on the banks of the river, and the report of his pact with the devil. God knew for what purpose, since the priest seemed to be a man without any ambitions, interested only in caring for his meager flock of the faithful. All these suspicions of madness and diabolic perversion, Veremundo said, were about to jeopardize the reverence and respect that the people of the neighborhood had always felt for their parish priest and his hitherto praiseworthy life. Father Aristides almost choked with laughter at all that nonsense. But he decided to stop the spread of this tale, which could, in fact, jeopardize his reputation, and to explain the mystery, which he immediately proceeded to do.

"The purpose of my pact, Veremundo, is clear and precise, and I shall reveal it to you. It is to satisfy my great sin. You know what a glutton I am, how I like to eat certain things, and of all the things I like, my greatest weakness has always been a good *guaiamu* stuffed with *farofa*, the way old Ana prepares it. *Guaiamu,* Veremundo, is the greatest temptation of my sin of gluttony. The purpose of my secret pact is to catch enough *guaiamu* to satisfy my greed; but it isn't a pact with the devil as people are saying. The devil has nothing to do with it, Veremundo. It is a pact made with this little devil, João Paulo, who is the best *guaiamu* catcher I have ever known in my entire life. It is a pact strictly between the two of us and till today a secret one. However, after what you have told me, it would be better to gather a small group of our friends, those who are closest to the church, and by explaining everything I will put an end to these stories."

Late that same afternoon, sitting in his rocking chair in the small living room and contemplating the picture of the heart of Jesus, Father Aristides, surrounded by a dozen pious men and women he favored, revealed the mystery of his strange excursions along the river banks, the excursions that had caused so much disquiet.

Leading the conversation as it pleased him, Father Aristides explained that he had always liked crabs. As a student in the seminaries of other lands, he had eaten different varieties of crab and appreciated them all, but when he came to Recife and first ate *guaiamu,* he realized that here was the finest variety of crab: the meat of its legs more tender and its fat entrails more spicy. The

54

priest attributed this superiority to the racial character of the *guaiamu* and its special diet.

The *guaiamu* is a variety of crab that does not like mire and, unlike other crabs, will not live in it. It prefers dry spots in the driest areas of the river banks. It does not smear itself with filth, as do other crabs. It does not have the color of mud. The *guaiamu* has a blue shell and blue eyes, as if it were representative of a superior breed, one well-born, well-bred, and well-fed.

"The *guaiamu* is an Aryan crab," said the priest, smiling, and he confessed to his closest friends that he had become so used to the delightful *guaiamu* that now he could no longer pass too many days without it. And since the *guaiamu* is considerably rarer and harder to catch than the ordinary crab, the priest ordered it from everyone, but sometimes days would pass without his being able to revel in his favorite dish. Then his pleasure in eating at all would diminish greatly.

It was by sheer luck that he came upon a solution to this tormenting problem—that of wanting to have *guaiamus* in abundance. Accidentally, he discovered a new and infallible method of catching the crab. He was also lucky to find in João Paulo the ideal assistant in the use of this new method.

Father Aristides went on explaining how, one hot day, while walking on the banks of the river, he suddenly was met by a great storm. It was one of those summer storms in which a violent rain falls abruptly, almost without previous warning, and is followed by strong winds and the tremendous roar of thunder. The priest crossed the field under the pelting rain, trying to escape the storm. It was then he saw a real mob of *guaiamus* running in all directions on the ground. They zigzagged in no particular direction since, from the minute the storm started, the crazed *guaiamus* had abandoned their holes and had run about aimlessly and insanely.

It was at that moment the priest imagined the most practical way of catching *guaiamus* would be by creating storms—small, man-made storms to rouse them. For this job the priest hired João Paulo. He found the boy one day catching a *guaiamu* with a stalk of grass that he would push into the crab's hole in order to attract it. Then the boy would withdraw the stalk very slowly, until he had drawn the *guaiamu* completely out of its hiding place.

That whole staging, including the drumrolls, the pouring of water, the unusual sounds that he produced in the field, were indispensable ingredients for the creation of artificial storms for the capture of crabs.

As his narrative ended, the priest invited his friends to attend one of these hunts the following day. Some of them had gone and returned enthusiastic. Soon the true story spread and serenity returned to the faithful of the church of Afogados.

From then on, when Father Aristides passed with his drum and his straw basket, accompanied by João Paulo with his watering can on his head, the people were no longer frightened. They greeted him respectfully and smiled; the women and children stopped to kiss his hand and then, from the side of the road, they watched those two peculiar figures with their strange equipment as they solemnly proceeded to their battlefield.

Today the sun was very hot and the sky was cloudless. The two walked side by side with their eyes halfclosed, dazzled by the excess of light. The priest moved forward with heavy steps, in constant danger of getting stuck in the muddy terrain, while João Paulo followed anxiously, forever changing sides, not knowing which direction the priest would take in his day's strategy.

The beauty of the day, the news received yesterday concerning forthcoming approval by the diocese of a grant for the thorough cleaning of the church—for a coat of paint and the removal of owls and bats from the ceiling—added to the turkey offered him a while ago, filled the priest's soul with an overwhelming joy this morning. He greeted everyone with a large smile accompanied by enthusiastic gestures, and as he reached an uninhabited area, the priest started to sing softly, a sacred hymn with a somewhat martial beat.

"Have you been going to your catechism classes, João Paulo?" asked Father Aristides, suddenly stopping his singing and placing his fat hand on the boy's neck.

"Yes, Father Aristides, I have," answered João Paulo without hesitation.

"Do you already know all the Commandments by heart, João Paulo?"

"Yes sir, Father Aristides, I know them."

"And you obey all these Commandments to the letter, João Paulo?"

"Yes I do, Father Aristides."

"Have you been saying your prayers every night before going to sleep, João Paulo?"

"Almost every night," answered the boy, with less conviction in his voice.

"And why not every night, João Paulo?" asked the priest in a reproachful tone.

João Paulo explained with difficulty that sometimes he was so tired, he fell asleep without fulfilling the sacred duty of thanking God for his daily bread, and without offering his body and soul to the Lord in case he should be called without warning by the Savior.

The truth of the matter was that João Paulo always tried to fall asleep before his parents retired because after they fell asleep the boy was always awakened with a start by the shrill notes of that macabre symphony that filled the hovel with strange sounds. In the middle of the night the boy often woke with a start from his nightmares to hear the fearful noises that shattered the silence of the later hours. Outside, the wind howled and entered through the cracks of the shack as if millions of flutes were playing. The rain tapped on the straw roof, and drops fell from the eaves into the mud.

From all over came the crazy dialogues between frogs and crickets, famished dogs and pigs, growling as they dreamed about food. But the most terrible of the noises, those that bothered João Paulo the most, were precisely those created in the night in his own hovel: the rough snore of Zé Luis, the tired hiss of his mother, and the periodic crackle of farts. Farts from all those swollen bellies distended by gases formed in abundance by that volatile mixture of crab meat and manioc flour, the almost exclusive diet of all these people. The crackling sound of the farts in the most diverse tones surpassed all the other sounds, including even the loud notes of the soloist of this nocturnal symphony, the bullfrog. That is because the farts burst with strident sounds the way the clatter of plates or the beat of a drum decisively shatters the most discreet and delicate sounds of the string instruments.

All this terrible gamut of noises crossed João Paulo's mind, but he dared not speak of these things to the priest, above all not of this ugly fart thing. His father always advised him to be careful not to let one escape in the priest's presence. That is why, when he walked with him, João Paulo stepped with great care, in a manner that justified the phrase of marshland urchins to describe a certain kind of walk. They call it "the-walk-of-holding-back-fart."

How could he now fail in respect by letting such an ugly word escape his mouth, by talking about farts to his priest? So he explained that when he did not sleep well one night, the next one he fell asleep immediately without having time to say his prayers.

At that moment they walked over an area where the

ground looked as if it were a mud toothpick holder, so full of crab holes was it. The priest looked at the ground, stopped, and the hunt began.

"We'll start here, João Paulo," said the priest, rolling up the sleeves of his cassock and freeing himself from his straw basket.

Immediately they started the beating of the drum that imitated thunder, and the priest began the hissing that reproduced the howling sounds of the wind. At a given moment the priest made a commanding gesture in the direction of João Paulo and the boy let rain pour from the watering can into the hole of the *guaiamu*. When the water hit the bottom of the hole, the dizzy *guaiamu* came out to the field. João Paulo chased the crab in his zigzag path and then, hurling himself to the ground, seized him.

All morning the make-believe storm thundered over the plain, and only at noon did the priest return home for lunch. His face was burning from the sun, his cassock was covered with dust, and his basket was filled with *guaiamus*. He put the *guaiamus* in a fenced enclosure, the *caritó,* which he had built back of his garden so old Ana could fatten them with the remains from the kitchen. Now the priest entered his dining room and got ready for lunch.

Tying the napkin around his neck, Father Aristides smiled in ecstatic delight as he saw the roast turkey—the turkey of Saint Sebastian, the martyr—steaming in a platter on the table. But before attacking the turkey, the priest was faithful to his habits and started his lunch with a plate of stuffed *guaiamus,* their shining blue shells the same color as his chinaware.

IV
of how the ground disappeared from under the rubber millionaire's feet . . .

The work João Paulo performed in the afternoon at the parish priest's house did not afford him the same pleasure as his morning task, *guaiamu*-catching on the river banks. When he helped to create storms to capture *guaiamus,* João Paulo saw himself grow in his own eyes and attain the height of the heroes of the fabulous stories told by his friend Cosme—stories of titanic fights for extraordinary treasures; of terrible battles against unknown enemies and supernatural monsters.

As João Paulo walked through the fields, he let his imagination take over, and there were times when the *guaiamus* grew and swelled to the size of monsters capable of swallowing a man like those snakes in the Amazon that, according to Cosme, can swallow an ox and then spend a whole month digesting it.

They became monstrous crabs that, after swallowing

men, proceeded on their way with their victims in the enormous trunks of their shells, protected by the gigantic legs lined up like weapons of war. But João Paulo was always ready to save the victims and battle victoriously against these imaginary monsters. He was always ready to free the prisoners from those living trunks, the crabs.

At his morning task, therefore, João Paulo always found something to remind him of heroic things. But in doing the insignificant household tasks—sweeping the garden, polishing furniture, removing cobwebs from the ceiling of the priest's house—João Paulo felt cheated, a little boy again, a hovel dweller, a priest's servant.

So as not to rebel against this humiliating work, the boy returned to dreamland. He let his arms and hands take care of the tasks, but his mind escaped and traveled through the world, seeing and doing extraordinary things. It was as if he were no longer at the priest's house, but at his friend Cosme's instead. He felt as if he were the legs that Cosme lacked, and as if the two of them were traveling together through all those places Cosme had gone in the days of his impressive adventures.

Cosme was the constant companion of João Paulo's imaginary adventures. That is because it was Cosme who, when they met, had sent him on his first trip to dreamland. They had been friends for three years now and their friendship had grown steadily.

This friendship started the day João Paulo was flying

a kite at the edge of the marshes and suddenly felt an insistent beam of light hit his face. Puzzled by this, João Paulo gathered his kite under his arm and moved toward the door of Cosme's hovel to find where the light was coming from. He saw nothing, because the window of the shack was higher than he was, but he heard a voice inviting him to enter. He opened the door and saw, stretched on a wooden cot, a thin man with very skinny legs and arms and a huge head from which hung a white beard. João Paulo had seen similar heads on the saints of the church of Afogados. He was afraid.

The man, however, smiled and made him sit on the little bench at his side. He explained that he had called him because he wanted to talk a little. He asked where the boy lived and who his father was. He showed interest in João Paulo's life and games. An hour later they were close friends. Cosme asked João Paulo to bring, whenever possible, the old newspapers he found in the city. Using the papers as an excuse, João Paulo's visits to the paralytic became more frequent.

The boy gathered newspapers from the garbage cans of the rich, from garden benches, and from drugstores and bakeries whose owners would kindly give them to him. Beaming, he would bring his load of old newspapers to his friend. At first João Paulo thought Cosme wanted these old papers to cover his crippled body during the cold nights. But Cosme explained the real reason:

that the hand-mirror and the newspapers were practically the same thing. With them he could communicate with life, could be informed of what was happening in the world. The mirror could tell him what happened right here in his little world; the newspapers could tell what happened farther away, in the city, in other cities, and in the great world.

During these visits, Cosme told the boy of his past adventures. Like Zé Luis, he too had been born in the backlands, in a small town of Seridó, a region that produces cotton with the longest fiber in the world. They say it is even longer than the Egyptian cotton fiber, already famous in the time of the Pharaohs. When he was a child, Cosme had worked as a janitor in a public school where he attended classes and learned to read. He read all the books in the school's library and became addicted to reading. As an adult, Cosme had established himself in his town as a cotton trader. He installed a small cotton gin and bought and sold the cotton produced in the region. In his case, it was not the drought that had caused his flight from the backlands. He had been able to survive several droughts. It was something much worse that forced him to leave.

"It was the monopoly," said Cosme, "which is a monster far crueler than drought. Besides, the drought comes and goes, and the people it expels can always return to their lands. It is not that way with monopoly. When monopoly comes and establishes itself in a region, it never leaves."

66

João Paulo, who did not quite understand the story, asked what monopoly was.

"Is it some bad disease?"

And so Cosme patiently explained everything to João Paulo. He told the boy that his business had been going well. He traveled in the neighborhood areas buying cotton from the planters. He would then remove the seed from the cotton and sell the fiber and seeds in the capital. He liked this business and the trips he took, on which he always bought many books.

One day a group of well-dressed young men appeared in the region. They came from São Paulo and their business was buying cotton. They offered the planters a price that Cosme could not pay, far higher than the market price. But he tried to meet their prices anyway. However, when he came to Recife to sell the cotton and seeds, it was for a much lower price, which made him lose a great deal of money.

During two crops he tried to fight the monopolists of the south but soon realized that it was impossible to compete with them. He could not understand how they could do business the way they did. He tried to establish contact with these men of the new cotton market. They were refined, well-bred, and friendly. They were pleasant and explained to him what was going on: they worked for a large foreign company that specialized in importing cotton and had decided to establish itself in the northeast. The company wanted no competitors and started to remove them from its path. Even the small businessmen like Cosme had to go. That is why the company paid a price above the market that small businessmen were unable to pay. The monopoly would purposely lose money for two or three years but in the end they alone would own the local cotton to market. And then they could set whatever prices they wished.

The young men explained to Cosme that the best thing he could do would be to abandon the field. Since they were his friends, they would arrange for the company to buy his small cotton gin. Cornered this way, Cosme had to give in. He emigrated from the backlands before his money ran out in the fight against this monster, the monopoly. He sold his workshop to the company, which took it apart, and then he left for the capital, Recife.

João Paulo still did not quite understand the issue and asked why the government did not defend him against this monster. Cosme answered that there was a good reason for this: the representative of the company in the state was the son of the governor, who was one of those who peacefully ate from the monster's hand.

Cosme then read in the Recife papers that men of courage were becoming rich overnight in the territory of Acre. The war in Europe had upped the value of rubber tremendously, and the Amazon was the rubber paradise. He was sorely tempted to go into such a venture, though more reasonable people tried to cool his enthusiasm. His former employer, Professor Guilhermino, said:

68

"Don't go to Acre. Acre is another world. It can be very good, but those who go there never come back."

But Cosme was young and ambitious and he went. He went and came back. But when he came back, he was a cripple, maimed for life. And now he lay, stretched on his cot, sadly recounting his adventures to the wide-eyed and dreamy João Paulo.

"I left Recife in a ship of the Costeira Line and traveled as far as Belém, capital of Pará. From there I went upstream to Manaus in a small river steamer. Together with other northeasterners migrating from droughts, I crossed that expanse of water in open-mouthed astonishment, after having lived in the arid backlands where never a drop was found. It was not necessary to go to Acre, because right there in Manaus I made a fortune. I went upstream on one of the branches of the river, taking with me my equipment and two men to help me collect rubber, and soon I started to make money. The money I made grew; it stretched as would a rubber band. From one day to the next I became more important. I bought only foods imported from Europe: canned meat, beans, vegetables, legumes and fruits, chocolates, and fine wines. The truth is that everything consumed in that region came from Europe. Meat and beans came from England. France sent champagne and also the comic actresses who sang in the theater of Manaus. Women came from Poland to fill the brothels. The state of Amazonas did nothing but produce rubber. No one did anything other than to collect the rubber or cure it or sell it and become rich fast."

Cosme saw João Paulo's growing interest in his eyes and so, as he caressed his hairy beard with his thin fingers, he continued:

"But misfortune walked faster than wealth in the Amazon. I was feeling on top of the world and then it crumbled before me. At that time, I was living with a blond Polish girl called Janine, who had a large black mole on her upper lip. She was a superb woman. I gave her several lengths of silk and a pearl necklace that I bought at the Japanese store. In those days I used to go regularly to the important carbarets of the city where I lit my friends' cigars with five-hundred-milreis bills. I was the one who raised the standing of the rubber trees tappers, the *seringueiros*. And so I was living like a lord, sure of myself and of the future, when one day, on the street as I left a cabaret, I suddenly felt the ground disappear from under my feet. At first I thought it was all the champagne I had drunk that made me feel weak in the legs, but it was not the drinking that I felt. It was beriberi coming up through my legs and taking over my entire body. It was paralysis caused by lack of fresh foods that on that night hurled me onto a bed from which I would never again rise to my own two feet. In my former arrogance I had felt as if I owned the world, and I never expected to be struck down by beriberi, though I had heard of thousands of other *seringueiros* who had been attacked by this strange disease. In those days no one knew what beriberi was, but today it is known to be a disease of hunger.

"So as not to leave my skeleton buried in the land of rubber, I hurriedly fled from that green hell. I bought a wheel chair at Antonio Mendes' furniture store. Antonio Mendes was becoming filthy rich by charging exorbitant prices for these chairs when he sold them to the *seringueiros* stricken by the paralysis. I came down the river again on a steamship with a crowd of them. Our wheel chairs were placed on the deck and we complained to one another about our misfortune, the end of all our illusions of becoming rubber millionaires. We were simply a pack of human rags thrown on the deck of that ship, returning disillusioned to our homes in an effort to save our skins."

Cosme told how, on his arrival in Recife, he had consulted all the celebrated men of medicine. These wise men told him that the disease was an intoxication produced by alcohol and spoiled food. To recover, he had, above all, to eat as little as possible. It was almost a constant fast. And while he fasted and the doctors ate up all the money he had so painfully saved, the paralysis progressed. And so his fortune had dissolved, as did the muscles of his legs, his strength, his ability to walk, and thereby, his power over others.

"If today I'm on this cot stretched out like a rag," Cosme would say as he moved his mirror in the palm of his hand, "it is my own fault. It is true that it was the poverty of the backlands that forced me to leave and the hunger for a fresh start in the Amazon that defeated me, but it was my ambition for wealth that lured me there and that was my damnation."

When João Paulo became acquainted with all the details of Cosme's odyssey and his unsuccessful adventures in the conquest of the world, the boy's admiration for his friend grew, as did his curiosity about the rest of the old man's life. And Cosme always satisfied the boy's curiosity. He told João Paulo about the wonderful things he had seen in the world he had traveled on foot, but he also told him of the world he had traveled with his mind and spirit. He related to the boy everything he remembered from his youthful readings. João Paulo was completely enraptured by the stories. For him, Cosme was a kind of oracle who knew everything and whose every word was sacred. And it was so not only for João Paulo, who was a little boy; almost everybody in Stubborn Hamlet regarded him equally highly. All admired Cosme's wisdom; he was the real brain of the community. His thoughtful mind judged their grave problems or explained things otherwise incomprehensible to their limited learning. As time went by, the muscles in Cosme's body shriveled, but the more they shriveled, the more his head seemed to grow and, with it, his knowledge.

Stretched on his cot, lying in his hut deep in the woods, it seemed as if Cosme were in permanent communication with the entire world. Everything that happened seemed to be translated to him immediately through mysterious fluids. In fact, he knew of things before they even took place. His learning made him a diviner, a kind of prophet in the eyes of the community. A year before, during one of his conversations with Zé Luis, Cosme foretold that Rosa, the single sister of Mateus, would become pregnant. And with a malicious smile he even added that her son would strongly resemble Sebastião. And yet no change was noticed in Rosa's life. When, months later, her belly started to grow, people thought Cosme had guessed it. But he denied it had been a guess. He modestly said that his mirror saw and told him things that were invisible to the eyes of neighbors. When a horrible crime of jealousy had occurred in the neighborhood and the body of the mulatto Júlio was found in the marshes, a knife in his groin, no one knew who the assassin was. But Cosme knew, because his mirror had seen the crime. And it was through his help that the police found the murderer.

João Paulo's mind was dwelling on the details of Cosme's life when he heard the priest calling him from the living room. He dropped the rake next to the garden wall and went inside. The priest told him to call the sacristan quickly and ask him to toll the church bells because he had just learned that Dona Clotilde, president of the Daughters of Mary, had suddenly died.

She had been one of the pillars of the church, its great benefactress. The bells should toll fast and loud.

73

João Paulo ran to the sacristan's house but did not find him. He had gone to town to get some candles for the seventh-day mass of another dead person. In the absence of the sacristan, the priest asked João Paulo if he knew how to toll the bells. The boy said he did indeed know how—that whenever the sacristan was lazy, he sent João Paulo up to the church tower to peal the bells and call the faithful to mass. As for the death toll, he had rung it more than a dozen times.

João Paulo climbed the church tower. From its height, at sundown, he saw the entire city in purple. On one side the houses grew in size until they became skyscrapers in the middle of the city. The church towers also rose steadily until they reached the great heights of the church towers in the city of Recife. On the other side the houses diminished in size and, as they receded in the distance, they became hovels and hutches, until they disappeared completely in the mire of the mangroves.

On top of the church tower João Paulo felt as if he were perched on the top of a mountain with streams flowing down both sides—the rivers of fortune on one side, the rivers of misery on the other. Some flowed to the land of the rich, others to the land of the poor. At this moment, João Paulo remembered a phrase he had heard from his mother:

"The other side is the paradise of the rich; this is the paradise of the poor."

And then, as he pulled the bell ropes in the death

knell he did it with a certain perverse pleasure, knowing that the sounds torn from the bronze would pierce the air in all directions and frighten the inhabitants of both the rich city and those of the miserable marshlands. They would all hide fearfully in their houses. If Cosme, in his hut, hearing the death toll, pulled the sheet that covered his body up to his neck, feeling the icy breath of death blowing over him, Colonel Vanderley, who lived in the luxurious mansion on the Largo da Paz, on hearing these funeral sounds, would also run in fright from the terrace and hide in his room in fear of being caught by death, which at that moment was hovering in the air.

João Paulo knew that in each house, be it poor or rich, when the death toll was heard, people would feel a cold shiver running down their spines, reminding them of the sword of death. In the house of the rich, where the fear of death was greater, the shiver was also more intense, as if the sword had already penetrated.

As the bell tolled, João Paulo laughed to himself, remembering that Cosme had once told him that the rich have tough and unbending hearts but weak nerves. And João Paulo pulled the ropes of the bell furiously, as if he were pulling on the weak nerves of all the rich. He pulled them harder and harder, hoping to shatter those nerves completely.

V

*of how
Zé Luis
spoke to God
without first
crossing himself . . .*

On nights when the moon was full, the neighbors would come over and sit in front of Zé Luis's hovel to exchange stories. If, like tonight, it was cool and there was a breeze heavy with the smell of gulfweeds, they would squat around a small fire built of mangrove twigs and warm themselves with the flames and an occasional drink of rum.

João Paulo leaned against the clay wall of the hovel and abandoned himself to the pleasure of listening to the stories. The pleasure was that much greater when it was his own father who told them, which happened rarely. Today was one of those great days. The fact is that Zé Luis was a man of few words, nor was he one who enjoyed confiding in others. On the contrary, he listened more than he spoke. Only rarely did he open up and reveal his more intimate feelings. Tonight the neighbors insisted that he tell how he ended up in the marshlands and how he came to Stubborn Hamlet. Zé Luis gave in. Perhaps it was to please João Paulo, whose bright eyes stared imploringly at his father. Had he not promised his son that one day he would tell his odyssey, which had started in the backlands and ended here in the marshlands? Well, he would do so today. And so Zé Luis began.

At first he stumbled on the words, only with difficulty overcoming the confusion of his memories. But then he took hold and his story flowed like a stream, over-whelming João Paulo's soul with happiness.

"Hunger is not something you talk about," began Zé Luis. "It is nothing but sadness—sadness and shame. It is an ugly story. But if you insist, I shall tell it to you anyway. I'll tell you about the sadness and shame we went through during the drought of 1947.

"Till then, we had lived happily in the arid region of Cabaceiras. It is true that this is the driest county of the northeast and that periodically we would be tormented by the lack of rain, but I always got along. When the drought caught you on one end, you found a way out somewhere else. If there was no more grass, we fed branches to the cattle. If there were no more branches, the cattle would be driven to a pasture at the foot of a mountain. There was always a way out. We would mix manioc flour with wild flour and flour of *macambira*. That, with some wild roots, would help us through the difficult period. It was hard work, there is no doubt, but it had its rewards.

"I tended Colonel Virgilio Maracejá's cattle and had a small farm. Of four calves born, one got my brand. That was my pay as a cowhand. In our little hut it was pleasant enough to live. When I returned home from work on the purple afternoons of the backlands, Maria would be sitting in the doorway nursing João Paulo. God forgive me, but seeing the boy in Maria's lap, I was reminded of the images of the Virgin Mary nursing the God-child. The older boy Joaquim played in the yard, and when he saw me in the distance, he ran to meet me. I was happy with my wife and two sons. But in 1947 things were really bad. I never saw a drought so terrible. There was nothing with which to fight it.

"Everything dried out, the valleys and the mountains, and news reached us that the drought was widespread. I tried everything, but couldn't cope with it. From dawn to sundown I would gather cactuses for the cattle to keep them from dying of hunger and thirst. It was no use. In a few weeks the cattle became paralysed from hunger. Their rumps stiffened and they couldn't walk. I think it was the same disease Cosme caught in the Amazon. I built a sort of sling of plaited leather straps and placed the cows on them on their bellies, but they died anyway, their bodies suspended and their heads and tails pointing to the parched ground. I ran

79

half-crazed in search of water that seemed to flee people the way the devil flees the cross. The water in the stone tank soon tried up. The water hole of Riacho Fundo, which held a brackish and muddy water, lowered with each thirsty migrant countryman. Soon it was nothing more than a dark hole with a little wet mud on the bottom that had to be squeezed in a strainer to give a few drops of water. And finally at the bottom there was just stone, and you can't draw blood from a stone. I then fetched water from a source at the foot of the mountains more than a league away. But the endless lines of migrants soon finished the last drop. And we started to die of thirst. Then the tragedy took place that robbed me of the love for my land."

Zé Luis paused, as if to breathe anew before pursuing his long story. He drank some rum, dried his lips with his sleeve, and went on:

"I remember that sad day well. I spent the whole afternoon digging the stone-hard ground at the edge of the parched lowland in search of a cassava root that by accident might have been left buried in the now-empty vegetable garden. But I found nothing. Discouraged, I sat on a stone by the parched brook and watched the barren and impressively large plain that surrounded me. The drought had killed everything. I was so depressed at the sight of stone and sand that I felt as if, within me, my heart had also turned to stone. I was overcome by a tremendous desire to let go and lay my heavy body on that hot, cruel land—to fall asleep, never to wake again. But I remembered Maria waiting for me to bring something and my son Joaquim who lay sick on his wooden cot. So I resisted my overwhelming depression. I cut a few pieces of *xique-xique* cactus with my knife and went home to try once more to placate the hunger of my family."

And so Zé Luis evoked for his listeners his great struggle against hunger and the threat of death. He told of how, walking on the rough roads, the corded soles of his canvas shoes hit the ground with the sound of a wooden rattle, and how his thoughts, too, started to rattle in his poor head. When would this terrible drought end? What would go first, the drought or his family? What would be better—to die of hunger and thirst in his own land, or to emigrate and die of fatigue and shame on someone else's land? Like a dusty ribbon, the road wound toward the edge of the valley where there was a hill with quince tree stems. Every now and then he would see a coarse wooden cross at the roadside, marking the spot where a wanderer had fallen dead of hunger and fatigue.

Before he reached home, the sun had already disappeared and an emberlike glare of blazing red covered the horizon, turning the landscape into a dismal bloody sight. At this moment of transition the whole earth seemed to grow and become empty and much too large. Zé Luis felt an infinite loneliness. As soon as he entered the house, he asked after his sick boy and Maria answered in terrible distress:

"The poor little one is burning with fever and dying of thirst. He asks for water all the time but I don't have even a drop left to give him. It's all gone."

Dropping his leather hat on the table, together with the sticks of cactus, Zé Luis grabbed a pitcher and left again in search of water. Knowing there was no water nearby, he went directly toward the house of Joca Salgado, who lived almost a league away. He went to ask for a glass of water to quench the thirst of his sick son. He knocked on Joca's door, which opened by itself. He entered and found no one there. He immediately realized that the whole family had left with the migrants. Striking a match, he ran to the kitchen and found an empty water jug turned downward in a corner. At that moment he felt a horrible tightening in his throat, as if the hateful thirst wanted to strangle him.

He ran in despair from Joca's house and through the deserted fields, and decided to emigrate also; to leave that cursed land that very same day—land on which a man worked every blessed day only to see at the end his son dying for want of a drop of water with which to quench his thirst. In the effort of walking through the barren plateaus, still daylight-hot, he felt his face covered with sweat. And as he passed his hand through his soaked hair he thought of the immense joy that a strong rainfall would give—one of those tremendous downpours that sometimes fall in the backlands, a downpour that would drench his clothes, his body, and go to the marrow of his bones. His desire was so great, his thirst so intense, and his anguish so deep, that he started to have hallucinations, and several times, in his perspiring confusion, he even stretched his hand out to the empty night air to see if it was not really raining. He entered the house like a lunatic and screamed to Maria:

"Get our stuff together, woman; wrap up the boys; we're leaving this cursed land. We're going down to the marshes where there will always be water for Joaquim and João Paulo!"

The woman who sat in the front room with her eyes on the cactuses, her shriveled chin resting on her shriveled hand, answered in a slow voice:

"Water won't help any more. Joaquim is dead."

Zé Luis shivered from the impact of the blow that at once dissipated all his hallucinations. He felt the terrible power of hate and revolt run through him from head to foot. He entered the room and saw the dead body of his son, a bag of bones with clear, wide-open eyes, wrapped in a patchwork quilt, on which the flame of a candle threw light shadows. Then Zé Luis turned his eyes to the window and through it to the yard of the farm, which looked as if it were a gigantic pit leading to infinity. He went toward the window and, staring at the tranquil sky, spoke to God:

"Something like this You don't see, but should one commit one tiny little sin, Your enormous eyes are on us!"

And Zé Luis concluded his story with his voice almost shaking with emotion.

"It was the first time I had spoken to God without first crossing myself! Next day we buried Joaquim, and the three of us, Maria, João Paulo, and I, left that burning hell."

The memory of all that suffering drained Zé Luis. He fell into a sad silence and no one insisted that he proceed that night in telling the story of his peregrinations to Recife.

VI

of how hunger turned Zé Luis, an honorable cowhand of the backlands, into a disgraceful cheese thief . . .

A long time passed before Zé Luis could continue the story of his descent from the backlands to the marshes. It was the night they celebrated the baptism of the son of Juvêncio, who lived at the edge of Stubborn Hamlet in a straw hut with a tile floor.

Zé Luis told the rest of the story to his many friends who had also come to the baptism and who now gathered in Juvêncio's hut on the luxurious tile floor. All the other huts in Stubborn Hamlet had floors of beaten clay; but Juvêncio, who for years had worked at a tile factory in Olinda, had brought home one tile every day. The guard would not make trouble because of one tile. So, patiently, one tile at a time, Juvêncio had managed to gather enough tiles to cover the entire floor of his front room and half of his bedroom. Another few months and his entire hut would have the floor of a palace; it would all be covered with tile.

Juvêncio himself asked Zé Luis to finish the story he had started the month before, of his descent from the backlands. Zé Luis had told about sadness but had said nothing about shame. This too would interest them, said Juvêncio.

Zé Luis did not accede immediately, but after a few sips of rum he loosened up and told the rest of the story:

"It is my belief that the ugliest act a man can commit is to steal what doesn't belong to him. It's to take something away from others behind their backs. As far as I am concerned, the worst thing you can call any Christian is a thief. Well, in the drought of forty-seven I was a thief. I stole food. And I stole it from a good man who didn't deserve to be robbed. But I shall tell everything the way it happened.

"You already know it was not ambition that made us leave the backlands; it was not the pursuit of money; it was the pursuit of life. It was to save the lives of my family that I came to the coast. We came in search of life, but here, too, what we found was death. There was so much death among the migrants that one felt they were actually attending their own funerals. They were like corpses walking to their graves. At the roadsides there were more crosses than trees. The road was like a one-way street to the next world. And when one

86

reached the settlements and villages, it was the dead who were the most hospitable."

Zé Luis described abandoned settlements through which they passed—ghost towns with not a living soul in the streets and wide-open doors banging in the wind, where nothing had grown but the cemeteries as they had filled with souls. There were walls, alleys, even gardens, but all the towns they passed through were heaps of misery. It was a kingdom of death. Only the dead were looked after; no thought was given to the living. Zé Luis and his family walked like ghosts in a procession, as other people joined them from all over the backlands to press onward to the marshlands in search of water and food.

"You who came to Recife from nearby don't know the torture of dusty roads in time of drought. Those roads seem endless; and so does the suffering. The backlander walks over barren fields with the sun beating on his back; hunger cries within him, and dust fills his eyes and nose; he eats bread kneaded by the devil. That's what was happening to us when we left the backlands during the drought."

Zé Luis told how, after several days of marching, they once more began to see people in the houses. In that area the drought had not been as harsh, and many of the peasants had been able to remain on their land. There were even villages with markets; but there were always armed policemen at both ends of the market to prevent the famished migrants from overrunning and looting the market, killing or being killed for a little moldy flour.

"One night we stopped at a house that had a spring beside it. It was the spring that attracted us," said Zé Luis. "After drinking fresh, sweet water we couldn't leave that spot. We had arrived late in the afternoon, but we remained daydreaming around the spring, drinking a mug of water occasionally, until the sun disappeared completely. That was when the owner of the house appeared and offered us shelter for the night.

"Late that night, as we lay in the kitchen, some outsiders came. We heard the clatter of hoofs and then the voice of the owner of the house speaking amiably with another man. Early next morning we met the guest. He was a friend of our host and had a farm at the foot of the mountain. He was coming down from the backlands with a load of cheese and moist brown sugar for a merchant in Caruaru.

"The man's name was Xandú. He was a simple and modest man. He took to us immediately. He told us, as we drank a cup of weak coffee in the kitchen, that he owned a little farm at the edge of the backlands but, since his land was at the bottom of the mountains, it never suffered the tortures of droughts. On his land there was a spring that had never in his lifetime dried up. It fed a brook that ran winter and summer, irrigating his crops of sugar cane, corn, and beans. Everything he had was on a small scale, it was true, but it was enough, said the man, to give his family a decent life. Xandú invited us to return to the backlands during the season of rains and stop at his farm. We promised we would because I wanted to see this miracle of a brook forever running in the backlands, even if it was only over a few armfuls of land."

When Zé Luis finished his coffee, he took his leave of Xandú and his host, whose name he did not recall, and left with his family through the back door to continue his trip. But Xandú, who was watching from the door, saw at once that they could not get very far.

"He saw that I could no longer stand. My feet were torn and the toes bled on the cord of my canvas shoes. Maria, with her swollen belly, looked like a brooding duck walking on eggs. The man felt sorry for us and called us back. He offered to take us on horseback to Caruaru. His horses were thin, tired little animals but, as he explained, the load also was small and light, and he was sure we could ride between the loads. I could ride on one of the horses, and Maria on the other with João Paulo riding behind."

And so, after helping the man load the animals, they left on horseback along the road, like rich people. The man led the way, Maria was in the middle, and Zé Luis was mounted on the last animal.

"Astride the packsaddle frame," Zé Luis went on, "with my two feet thrown ahead at each side of the horse's neck, I felt comforted after all my sufferings. I felt like a lord riding over his own lands. The other migrants watched us with envy as we rode along."

João Paulo, listening attentively to his father's tale, vividly remembered that trip with his family on Senhor Xandú's horses. He even remembered his fright when, as it grew dark, he woke from a nap to see a huge jaguar mounted on the croup of the horse ahead, ready to devour him. He had screamed with terror. But it was no jaguar—only the horse's tail, raised as the animal performed its normal excretory functions without bothering to stop.

There had been so much talk of jaguars on the edge of the mountain that João Paulo had been overwhelmed by fear. Now he remembered how frightened he had been and how ashamed when everybody made fun of him for screaming in terror.

"From horseback the world looked different. The dust was not so thick and the sun did not seem so hot on our backs," continued Zé Luis. "Only the hunger was the same. With every jolt of the horses on the rough road, our stomachs growled like the belly of a pig. The sound of our empty insides was frightening. The heat brought forth a strong smell from the goods we were carrying. From the right came a good cheese smell that tickled my nostrils, from the left the nauseating smell of moist brown sugar that turned my stomach. It was the smell of curds that tempted me, and so I bent over a little to that side. The hunger in my empty belly grew stronger. My mouth filled with saliva, but the more I spat, the more my mouth filled up. Saliva even ran from the corners, and the smell of cheese was making me drunk and tempting me like the strong smell of a woman. I tried to resist the temptation, I thought of the man's kindness and of the favor he was doing us. I shouldn't touch his cheese.

"If the man had entrusted his load into my hands, the load was sacred and it was my duty to resist the temptation.

"I took some of the straw covering the cheese and started to suck on a dry stalk that held the good smell of cheese. In this way I thought I could dry my mouth and allay my hunger; but, far from quieting down, the hunger became even more compelling. Half wild and hardly aware of what I was doing, I started to lightly finger the soft balls of cheese. Suddenly, with my hand shaking like a criminal's, I stuck my fingers into one of the cheeses and pulled off a large chunk. I put it all in my mouth and started to chew carefully, trying to spread it around. I tried not to move my lips so that if the man turned around he wouldn't catch me eating his cheese. I kept my hand in the basket to soften the cheese, occasionally pulling a new piece off. The taste of cheese in my mouth increased my appetite even more. The more I ate, the more I wanted. It was like a vice, impossible to break. And from the time the sun rose until it sank in the sky, I continued, like a rat, chewing on the cheese.

"The horses ate earth from the road and I ate pieces of cheese," continued Zé Luis. "Occasionally the man spoke loudly, asking me questions. I closed my eyes, feigning sleep because my mouth was filled with cheese and I was unable to talk. He gave up chatting. But whenever he tried, my guilt increased. I tried to leave the rest of his cheese alone. I was unable to face the man, and I was afraid that before we parted he would find out that I had shamelessly devoured his cheese. I hoped that he would only notice the fact in my absence, after we reached Caruaru. I would leave him before. I would make up an excuse and would linger on the road until he was out of sight. But, as it had been hard on the previous day to part from the well, so it seemed impossible now to abandon the cheese."

The people laughed and their mouths watered as they heard this story about the cheese. João Paulo, open-mouthed, dribbled with pleasure at his father's tale. Zé Luis proceeded:

"I continued to eat cheese until I started to feel utterly stuffed. I felt very sleepy and must have dozed off. I'm not quite sure, but I suddenly felt tossed in the air, as if someone had pushed me from below, and I fell full force on the ground next to the horse. I looked at the load and saw it turned toward the side of the brown sugar. I then realized that I had eaten so much cheese that the load had become unbalanced. Everyone was alarmed at the noise of my fall. Maria screamed and Xandú hurriedly dismounted to see what had happened. I tried to explain that I had dozed off, but I couldn't talk straight since my mouth was still full of cheese. And when the man lifted the load in his arms to balance it, he saw everything. He saw the basket with sugar heavy as lead and the one with cheese light as a feather. I have never felt more ashamed in my entire life. The man yelled at me furiously, calling me thief and cheese robber to my face. Maria started to cry. The frightened boy also bellowed at the top of his voice. As I am not a man to take an insult and swallow it, I was overcome by a violent need to react. I got up from the ground, blinded by the desire to grab the man by his throat; but I just couldn't. He was in the right. I stood before him motionless, overwhelmed by his insults and my guilt. Confused, the man finally left, beating his horses and yelling at them. The last one had his load hanging over to one side, almost dragging on the ground. I didn't react, but my innards did, and till sundown I stood by the road under a *joazeiro* tree vomiting curds."

VII

*of how
Senhor Maneca
almost melted away
in his diarrhea caused
by hunger . . .*

The night of the baptism of Inácio, the son of Juvêncio Baraúna, was a memorable one. It was memorable because of the amount of rum in which the guests drowned their sorrows; and it was also memorable because of the stories told by some of these guests. It was not only the story of Zé Luis's descent from the backlands which that night became registered in the annals of the marshes. Another story also caused a sensation and is talked about to this day. It was the story told by Senhor Maneca from Crato.

When Zé Luis ended his story, Senhor Maneca said in a low voice:

"You, Zé Luis, vomited all your hunger out of shame, whereas I, excuse my language, I dropped my hunger all the way from the backlands to here."

The sentence shocked the listeners who were accus-

95

tomed to Senhor Maneca's seriousness. Straight-faced, with thin lips and bones almost visible, Senhor Maneca, unaware of the shock he had created, calmly proceeded with his story:

"I left the backlands only when I could no longer hold on. I ate up my reserves of corn and flour. Then I turned to roots. For an entire month I dug the hard ground parched by the drought, in search of roots of wild plants. I ate *xique-xique, macambira,* and roots of *mucunã,* a leguminous plant. I would still be eating these wild plants today so as not to leave my land were it not for my desperate thirst. It was thirst that expelled me from the backlands rather than hunger."

And Senhor Maneca's gaze wandered through the badly lighted front room as if trying to rebuild vividly in his mind the desolate landscapes of the backlands hardened by drought. It was as if right there in Juvêncio's hovel he saw the thirst of the ground, of the stones, trees, animals, and men. Everything covered by dry dust, a sort of concentrated thirst. Wetting his dry lips with his tongue, Senhor Maneca proceeded, but he was in no hurry to finish his story.

"When I felt that thirst would truly skin me alive, I decided to quit. I left Crato with a crowd of people heading toward the São Francisco River to catch a river steamer that would bring us to the marshes. It was a caravan of desperate men. The migrants, with death dogging their footsteps, had their throats tightened by thirst, clogged by the dust of the roads, and their entrails corroded by the wild foodstuffs they had consumed. But nothing was worse than the general diarrhea caused by hunger in all those people. They would crouch everywhere along the road without the slightest inhibition, writhing with cramps. Some, in their agony, would remain in one spot, rolling their contorted bodies in their own excrement. But most fought against it and continued to march forward. In the parched air of the backlands excrement dried fast and, turning into dust, entered our nostrils and increased our thirst.

"Here and there we would find a settlement. They were camps for transients organized by the Department of Droughts. From afar we would detect their presence by the putrid smell carried by the wind. It was a smell of human flesh in decay; a smell of putrescence, hunger, and death. I always avoided these camps where sickness lay in wait for victims. I passed them by, keeping my distance."

Juvêncio's hovel held an atmosphere of suspense. The rum bottles stood untouched on the little room's table, and the glasses remained on the floor next to each guest. Everyone was transfixed by Senhor Maneca's words:

"As I said before, it was a journey made by desperate people. I saw and heard things to break one's heart. I met a group of migrants from a village in Seridó who told me that they had been driven out of their houses by bats and snakes. Tortured by hunger and finding no more cattle from which to draw blood, the bats attacked people, sucking their blood while they slept.

Rattlesnakes too, excited by hunger and heat, came into the houses for their victims and lay under beds and tables ready for their deadly strike."

Seeing a flicker of doubt in the look of some of his listeners, the backlander's pride was hurt, and he changed his tone of voice and spoke faster and more harshly:

"If you choose not to believe, then don't, but I tell you that I saw with my own eyes the bat toothmarks on the skin of the men who told this story to me. And with these same eyes I saw the tears running down the cheeks of a woman who had in her own house lost both her sons from rattlesnake bites. They were twins and had already learned to walk at the time the drought started, but with all the starvation they returned to crawling and it was while they crawled over the floor of the house that the snakes caught both of them. Hearing stories like that, and writhing in pain, I finally reached the banks of the São Francisco River where I took the steamer named *Alagoas*. I remember it well because, as I arrived at the dock, I saw the name written in white letters on the brown hull of the ship, where the paint had all peeled off as if it too had suffered the horrors of the drought. We were in Pirapora. . . ."

"Pirapora, Senhor Maneca, why, that's Juvenal's village! He owns the brickyard of Imbolé," commented Juvêncio excitedly.

"Is Juvenal from Pirapora? I didn't know that. It must be a good place. I have nothing to say against it. I had even thought Pirapora would be the end of my torment. As soon as I boarded the ship, I hung up my hammock on the deck that was crowded with migrants and collapsed into it. I felt like another person. As soon as the boat started down the river, my will to live returned. But it was a passing illusion. The bell rang, calling everyone to dinner. All those famished people attacked the food like ravenous wolves. They ate with their mouths and with their eyes, but few finished their meal. In the midst of it, they would dash toward the stern of the ship. It was general chaos there. I thought at first that it was the so-called seasickness, and that they were returning through their mouths what their stomachs rejected. But it wasn't that. I understood what it was when I myself felt, as violently as ever, the tightening cramps in my bowels. I also dashed from the table in search of a latrine. They were on the ship's stern, and there were only four. The line of candidates was unending. Then, gradually the line broke up by itself. The men relieved themselves right there on the sides of the deck, holding on to the iron bars of the ship. I did the same.

"During the whole trip people were crouched on the deck which turned into a real pigpen. No one with bowels as corroded by wild plants as ours were could eat normally. We didn't even look like humans traveling. We were like pigs wallowing in our own dirt. When I left the ship in Penedo, I looked at the stern of the boat, so as to engrave her name in my mind. The name was illegible. The letters were all smeared, covered by the dirt that had run from the deck down the hull."

Senhor Maneca's listeners were repelled by his words and spat on the mosaic floor. Each grabbed his glass of rum but Senhor Maneca proceeded, indifferent to the surprise and repugnance of the crowd.

"It isn't over yet. There is more misery." He also gulped down more rum to clear his throat and continued his story:

"My intention was in fact to remain by the swamps and wait for the day when the rains would again fall in the backlands, so that I could return to my land. I had no intentions of abandoning it entirely, but there was nothing to do but settle in the zone of sugar-cane plantations until the drought let up a little. As soon as I reached that zone I was startled. I descended the mountains and there I saw in the valley a huge green sea. I thought I had reached the shore and that this was all water. It wasn't. It was a sea of cane. There was no end to the cane. I had never seen such a colossal plantation. I was frightened. In the midst of that sea of cane, right next to the mill, was a large white house with a chimney taller than the tower of the church of Carmo. It was a beautiful place. There was a small lake facing the house, and an orchard with fruit trees right next to it. Everything was clean and glittered in the sun.

"I offered myself for work there, but was immediately told to forget it. The owner of the mill wouldn't hear of migrants from the backlands. He hated them because once a famished group of migrants had invaded his warehouse. He now had two of his men standing at the warehouse door to greet the migrants with bullets. That was what the local people said. And even worse. They said that the water of the lake, apparently so quiet and so green, had in its depths the bones of many a migrant whom the man had ordered to be slaughtered in revenge for the time when some had eaten his beans and flour without paying for them. Such barbarity could only have been stories made up by these people who wished to scare me away from the place."

"They're no stories, Senhor Maneca. Of that I assure you. It's all true," said Zé Luis. "I know the place you mention and the owner of it very well. He is the Colonel Australiano from the Estrêla mill. The man is a beast. His cruelty is notorious all over the south of the state. Can you imagine that he still has hanging on the wall of his office two large ox horns with metal tips on their ends? The man says they are to give nettle and pepper enemas to any of his men who get out of hand. And they really are for that. I met two backlanders who worked for him. One day they decided to be tough and ask for a raise. They left Estrêla mill with their rear ends on fire from the pepper and hot-grease enema they got."

"Well, then, Zé Luis, you show that I was right in taking the precautions I took," continued Senhor

Maneca. "For safety I maintained my distance from that ill-famed house and settled under an *umburana* tree at the curve of a road. It was right then that two backlanders brought someone in a hammock and stopped to rest under the shade of the same *umburana* that was, in fact, quite inviting. And it was the conversation I had with these two young men that made me avoid that place and continue on the road until I reached Recife."

"And what was the conversation with the young men about, Senhor Maneca?" asked the now-curious Zé Luis.

"I will repeat the conversation bit by bit, and you will then tell me if I was right to leave. I asked the men, 'What are you carrying wrapped in that hammock, brothers?' And they answered, 'We carry a dead body, brother.' So I asked, 'Where does this dead man come from, brothers?' And they answered, 'From very far. In life he lived on the shoulders of the mountains and now, dead, he has been traveling for hours to his last dwelling place in the depth of the valley. He hurries no longer, nor is he impatient any more, as he was in life, brother.' 'Was he killed or did he die a natural death?' 'That is difficult to answer, brother. It seems more to have been a murder.' 'How was the man killed? With a knife or a bullet, brothers?' I asked. 'It was neither a knife nor a bullet; it was a much more perfect crime. One that leaves no sign.' 'Then how did they kill this man?' I asked, and they calmly answered: 'This man was killed by hunger, brother.' Now, you tell me, is this or isn't this enough to raise the hair on the head of a Christian?" asked Senhor Maneca as he ended his macabre tale on the tile floor of Juvêncio's hovel.

Senhor Maneca's companions considered him something of a poet, but they did not laugh about his story. To be honest, there was nothing to laugh about.

VIII
of how the headstrong dwellers of Stubborn Hamlet built their small town . . .

When Zé Luis and his family came to live in Recife, Stubborn Hamlet did not yet exist. At that time all that existed in the area was a large circle of mire that the river never covered, not even during high tides. Upon this muddy circle and in the midst of the mangroves of the marshlands four or five dwellers had built their huts, quite distant from one another, each one isolated and lost in that huge miry estate. The property was then shared by the shacks of Cosme, the Negress Idalina, Mateus the Red, and Chico the Leper, who had been the first to come to this wilderness.

Chico had moved there fleeing the society of men, and hiding to defend his freedom that was threatened by organized charity. Chico had caught leprosy and he knew it was enough for anyone to see his face, with his deformed nose and the huge fallen ears, to recognize his frightening illness. When the doctors wanted to examine him in a hospital, he adamantly refused, as he was not willing to give up his liberty in exchange for a remote cure in which he did not believe. When the visiting ladies of the Department of Public Hygiene came to see him in order to insist that he be checked at the hospital, Chico disappeared completely from Ambolê, where he had lived until then, and hid in the mire of the marshlands of Afogados.

At that time there were as yet no laws to protect ownership of a piece of land settled in this way, and the place was soon invaded by other settlers who came from distant places in search of a free piece of ground on which to put down roots. They were fugitives from other droughts, driven out of the backlands by burning winds and heaped up as human residue. They were emigrants expelled by the sugar plantations that were much better protected by law and on which invasions from other areas could not take place. There it was real slavery; the work in the cane fields was exhausting, with no time or permission for a man to raise a single stalk of corn or beans to help appease the hunger of his family. And so, the great sugar estate released its surplus of people that the great swamp estate absorbed as avidly as if it were blotting paper. And the city of Recife, soaked in the thick ink of misery that formed its crust of hovels, gradually swelled.

Meanwhile, the city of Pernambuco was fast becoming a metropolis of hovels. The governor of the state, in

106

defense of the threatened esthetics of his city, started a great campaign against hovels—a campaign against this urban leprosy that endangered with sordid spots of misery the seignorial beauty of the capital of the northeast and the pure and refined nobility of its ancient mansions and estates. In his campaign against the hovels, the governor made no effort to look for the real roots of the evil. He thought they were planted right there in the mire of the marshlands and that it would be enough to pull them out in order to end this wild outgrowth of hovels. Neither he nor his assistants seemed to realize that this rank overgrowth of hovels, which sprouted like mud flowers in the midst of the marshlands, had roots that spread all over the country, as well as in the substratum of its archaic social structure. It was the product of the agrarian feudalism that for centuries had oppressed and exploited those poor people who, in the end, preferred the stench of the marshes to the stench of the huts of the sugar mills and of the new shanties around the modern plantations.

It was part of the governor's campaign not only to destroy all the shacks set up at the city lines or by the main roads but, and above all, to enforce the ban against construction of new ones. Only the construction of tile-roofed houses was permitted—houses like those being erected by the social welfare agencies for the laborers protected under the law. But the governor forgot that the dwellers in the hovels were not laborers. They were, overwhelmingly, the unemployed who lived by their wits, or by odd jobs, or in the last resort, by crab-bing. That was why only the marshlands and the hovels fitted their means. In the marshes, the land belonged to no one. It belonged only to the tides. When the water rose and spread, it drenched the whole land, but when it receded, it left bare the high points. On these humps the migrants built their hovels, whose walls were made of mangrove branches and clay. The roof was made of coconut palm fronds or dry grass, or other materials found in trash piles. The materials were free and quite available, and the migrants lived in frank comradeship with nature. The marsh was a great companion and friend, furnishing everything: lodging and food, hovel and crab. It was not easy, therefore, for people of such restricted means to break with the marshlands merely to obey the law.

The first reaction was to stop building shacks near the city, and to start building them instead in more dis-tant spots like those where Zé Luis, Cosme, and Chico lived. Thus that almost-deserted area filled rapidly with so many hovels that it attracted the attention of the police. The latter had to act energetically because they had been formally instructed to do so by the superior authorities. They had to eliminate the leprosy of the hovels from the land.

These instructions came about because new owners appeared on the marshlands, which up to now had be-longed only to the tide. The new owners, by a strange coincidence, were important gentlemen and well connected. Since they were pillars of the local government, the local government supported them unconditionally, and from this same government they demanded total vigilance over these lands, ownership of which, through various unorthodox procedures, they had entered in the registry of submerged lands. These profiteers often registered nonexistent lands, hoping that someday the tide would release them. Others registered small islands already surrendered by the tide but barren and as yet not covered by the vegetation of the marshlands. They registered small circles of mire, islands resembling fetuses, with their soft, smooth bodies still wet with the nourishing slime of the river. These profiteers knew that the circles of mire would grow and that the mangrove, the creator of lands, would lift these humps of earth, fatten them, furnish them with the bones of its wrinkled roots, and turn them into fresh, green islands firmly anchored in the midst of the fruitful waters. They became proprietors of these lands in order to exploit them in the future, and they demanded exorbitant rents from the marsh dweller for the sliver of mire on which he had set up his hovel. And should the tenant be unable to pay, he would have to leave this mud already dried by the marshlands and go to another spot where the mire was softer, and live there in the water with the crabs. Many of these profiteers had once been poor wretches themselves: miserable, dirt-ridden, often, like their victims, born in the mud of the marshes; they had later been able to raise their heads up as a result of stinking transactions made in the mire of politics. Now important men, they had no second thoughts about stifling these wretches and twisting their necks. This they did with the same indifference with which the necks of dying gamecocks are twisted after the cock-fight, so they can die faster.

However, to spare their weak nerves, the profiteers charged the police with the task of twisting the marsh dwellers' necks in order to help them die of hunger. The law then sent inspectors to stop the construction of new hovels. The inspectors would drive stakes into the ground and warn everyone that beyond that point no one was allowed to build. Terrible threats were made— threats to tear down any new shack built beyond the stakes. They even threatened to burn down the entire settlement. But the hovels continued to appear, and that is why the region was given the name Stubborn Hamlet: because it stubbornly continued to exist and grow against the will and the orders of the government. Those people had guts! But the battle was fought with such shrewdness that it deserves to be told in detail.

The dwellers started by consulting Cosme, who had already revealed himself to be a counselor wise in judgment. Cosme explained that in his opinion this campaign against the hovels was a temporary one. It was nothing but a political maneuver of the government, a gimmick for winning next year's elections. It was pure demagogy. The truth of the matter was that the government was not popular and needed desperately to improve its prestige. With the cost of living so high, everyone was disgruntled. Even the wealthy were dissatisfied with the governor, because their businesses had not prospered much during his term. Trade was slow. The sale of sugar and cotton produced a low margin of profit. As for the people, they hated the government, particularly after the atrocities committed by the head of the police department against the employees of a textile factory that had gone on strike for higher wages. Instead of more money, the workers were severely beaten and their union leaders thrown behind bars. To further weaken the position of the government there was the opposition. In their electoral campaign, they took advantage of every rally to complain at the tops of their voices about the high cost of living and the miserable housing conditions of Recife. It was in the face of these circumstances that the governor organized a campaign carefully aimed at raising the government's prestige. He spoke to representatives of the federal government, mobilized the social welfare agencies, and launched a plan for popular construction works and low-cost housing for the poor.

All this, according to Cosme, was only a front. Half a dozen houses were built along the road leading to the city, especially the road leading to the airport, in order to impress out-of-town visitors with the huge accomplishments of the government. The rest would remain on paper, on the blueprints or the engineers' plans, or in the newspapers of the official press. The campaign against the hovels would last only until the elections anyway, and then everything would return to what it had always been: the poor, in their hovels, would be forgotten and the new government would help its friends to become richer. There was no time for anything else.

This explanation of Cosme's was not accepted unanimously. Among those present was a backlander called Januário. He worked for a man of prestige in the government, the local representative from Areias. He shyly ventured to suggest that perhaps the government was not that bad, that perhaps its intentions were even good, and that perhaps soon they would all be living in the new houses being built along the road to the airport. But Cosme burst out laughing at the naïveté of this peasant who believed in all the baloney handed out by the government. The houses were good only to further fill the pockets of the government contractors and, once ready, would be used to pay off political debts. These were no houses for them, poor hovel dwellers, who lacked prestige and influence in the machinery of government.

Cosme was used to campaigns to attract voters on the eve of elections. He was wise to these maneuvers. And even if the campaign were being undertaken with good intentions, as Januário stated, soon things were bound to take a different turn. The shrewd would corrupt those good intentions. Cosme reminded the group of what had happened during the government of

President Epitácio Pessoa. He was a man of the northeast. Born in a city in the state of Paraíba, close to the city in which Cosme himself was born, President Epitácio had been a man of good intentions. He had wanted to save the northeast from the calamity of droughts. He had gathered the best engineers of the country and had drawn a comprehensive plan for the construction of dams and roads: the Public Works for the Prevention of Droughts. He bought loads of machinery from foreign countries to carry out these tasks, and employed hoards of people.

And things began to happen in the northeast.

But difficulties soon arose. The bulk of the money sent by the federal government went directly into the pockets of those who pull the strings in politics, and the works did not progress. And when, after a tremendous failure and a huge scandal that the opposition made the most of, Epitácio left the government and the Public Works for the Prevention of Droughts fell into oblivion. All that machinery for digging wells, water holes and dams was abandoned in the fields and disintegrated like the carcass of a drought-killed ox.

Except for Januário, everyone agreed with Cosme. In fact, in the end even Januário agreed, as he no longer insisted on defending the government and his boss. The story really was as Cosme had told it. There was no hope of their leaving the marshes and their hovels. What was necessary at the moment was to hold tight to the hovels and not let them be torn down, so as not to

113

end up in the street at the mercy of wind and rain. It was important to draw a plan to prevent such a calamity, and they entrusted this task to the wise Cosme.

Cosme accepted the leadership. Tied to his bed by paralysis, he directed the battle of Stubborn Hamlet from there. He outlined a complete battle plan that, carried out to the letter, brought him total victory over the forces of the government and the police.

It was established from the beginning that new shacks would be built only one day a week, or rather, one night, since all construction work would have to begin at sundown and end that same night before dawn. And so it was done. During the week, all the residents joined in their efforts to gather construction material. Some would bring old boards from the city, others old zinc sheets and empty tin cans. There were those who were charged with cutting branches from the mangroves, and those who gathered coconut palm fronds, for which they climbed the trunks of trees on the shore. When there was a signal that the guards of the coconut plantations, armed with rifles, were approaching the area, the palm cutters flew from the crowns of the coconut trees with two large fronds, one under each arm, and landed in the loose sand of the beach like sea birds. All that material, coconut palms, mangrove branches, clay, kerosene cans, and sheets of zinc plate were piled in strategic spots hidden in the thickets of the marshlands.

On the day of construction the nervous tension grew

throughout the district. All had their ears cocked, listening, and they were impatient for the night to come so they could start work. Jobs were assigned. There were those who had to work on construction and those who would participate in the spectacle organized to distract the attention of the authorities. At dusk, in another end of the neighborhood far from where the new shacks would be built, the preparations for an all-night party would begin—for the *pastoril* (popular dramatic show with dances), the *maracatú* (carnival dances) or the *bumba-meu-boi* (traditional folk drama). It was usually the *bumba-meu-boi* that produced most enthusiasm in everyone, although the *maracatú* was noisier and better muffled the sounds of construction. When the arena was surrounded by villagers, mostly women, the ox would appear and sing:

"Vem meu boi lavrador	Come my plow ox
Vem fazer bravuras	Come show your tricks
Vem dançar bonito	Come dance nicely
Vem fazer mesuras	Come take big bows.
Vem dançar meu boi	Come dance my ox
Aqui no terreiro	Here on the yard
Que o dono da casa	For the owner of the house
Tem muito dinheiro."	Has lots of money.

The ox, in reality just a good dancer—usually Sebastião, his head covered by a cardboard structure with huge horns—danced, jumped, pirouetted, and bowed, following the orders of the cowboy. Once in a while he would stick his horns into the buttocks of someone in the audience, usually someone Sebastião did not like very much. And the fun would go on, "Hello, my ox!" to which the chorus would answer, "Eh! *Bumba!* Dance gracefully! Eh! *Bumba!* Make a big bow! Eh! *Bumba!* Scatter the crowd! Eh! *Bumba!*"

Each time the bass drum resounded, the construction workers were screened by the noise of the party and could perform their work undisturbed.

They began by pulling out the poles inserted by the inspectors and planting them sufficiently farther on so as to create "legal" space for the buildings. They would then push the stakes into the mud, hammer the nails in the rods, and fill the space between the rods with mud. It was as if they worked in velvet, making no sound, because the noise of the distant *bumba-meu-boi* screened the sounds of construction. If by chance an inspector would appear in the vicinity, he was surrounded by interesting chatter in the square, and the ox would bow deeply to impress him. If he was overzealous in the fulfillment of his duties and wanted to scour the neighborhood to see if the people were building something in a remote spot despite the night, then two figures, well instructed in their tasks, would enter the scene. They were two dark mulatto girls, very similar in looks, who worked for the Caxias cigarette factory. They would smile at the authority and insist that he let them show him around the city—that is, around the areas farthest from the one in which the construction was taking place. The authority usually fell into the trap and, telling coarse jokes, would follow the girls of Cosme's counterspy service.

But these men did not get far, either with Clotilde, the older one, or with Zita, the younger. The girls knew how to defend themselves from these powerful men and their daring propositions. They were always together, enticing, provoking, increasing desire, but always coming out safely. At most, they would offer their mouths and the nipples of their breasts, but they defended the rest obstinately. They gave just enough to distract the guardians of the law from their work.

And so construction would continue till morning. By the time dawn's first color appeared in the sky, the construction gang had finished its task. It had filled the empty space between the line of houses and the new stakes pushed into the ground. Hurriedly they would hide the remaining material for next week's work, bathe in the river, and go home.

As soon as the sun came out, new representatives of the law arrived. There was always a more suspicious one who would notice something—that the front hovels had a different façade or that the clay was very fresh— but the stakes were there in the ground as undisputable symbols that the orders had been obeyed and the authorities respected.

The law is to be respected but not obeyed, said Cosme contentedly as Stubborn Hamlet continued to grow.

IX

*of how João Paulo
came to know
his neighbors
better through Cosme's
little mirror . . .*

Stubborn Hamlet grew. The hovels now spread in all directions, even to the water's edge. The village looked like a heap of black gourds brought in the stream by the tide and strewn over the marshlands. Through the network of streets walked a whole crowd of people unknown to João Paulo. What was odd, however, was that Cosme knew almost everyone. Not that he had seen all of them closely, nor had he spoken with them. No, he knew them from a distance. He knew the images that his mirror brought him while they passed on the road. But each image was rounded out by precise information obtained through God knows what means. It is true that the older dwellers of the region visited him frequently. They came over for a chat every Sunday and holiday and kept him posted on the changes that took place in the hamlet, on the new faces, on the events of significance to that society, and on births and deaths.

It was through Cosme that João Paulo came to know all these people better, or at least those with more unusual stories, stories that deserved more detailed narration on the part of his friend. Late in the afternoon João Paulo, returning home from work, usually stopped at Cosme's hovel and stayed until suppertime. As they talked, the paralytic would "fish" for images in his little hand-mirror. When an image interested him, he called it to João Paulo's attention. It was during these afternoon "fishing expeditions" that João Paulo became acquainted with the drama of two characters who, like Chico, had moved to the zone of the hovels in order to hide in their dark barracks, as crabs hide in their holes. These characters were Mateus, the Red, and the Negress Idalina.

Mateus was the peaceful, relaxed type. He spent his life seated at the door of his hovel weaving fishing nets. However, he had come to Stubborn Hamlet in terrified flight from the police. Not that his hands had ever committed any crime so far as he could remember or of which his conscience could accuse him. His only crime was really that of having been born with hair of a color different from that of the other inhabitants of his place of origin. Mateus was born with flame-red hair.

He had never known his parents but there were steady rumors that he was the son of a German sailor who used to frequent a street of prostitution during the calls of his ship at the port of Recife. Mateus did not talk about the subject. Nor had he since childhood ever protested or become angry when, because of his flame-red hair, people had called him the Red. He was proud of this nickname and he never imagined that the un-usual color of his hair would create so many complica-tions in his life. He was working for a paper factory in Jabotão when these complications started.

It was a period of great social disquiet. Jabotão was the great center of agitation among workers in the northeast, the greatest center of Communist turmoil in the country. The well-to-do classes did not even call it the city of Jabotão. They called it *Moscouzinho,* little Moscow, so large did Communist influence in this city appear to loom.

It is true that Mateus was unaware of all this, and concentrated on his job in the factory. But by dint of circumstance he became involved in the controversy—in a battle with the police alerted against and fearful of agitators thought to threaten the national safety.

Through questioning carried out by the police in the working-class circles, the authorities occasionally heard a reference to the name Mateus, the Red. Perhaps there had even been direct mention of his name to the police, a fact that could have arisen from the type of greeting other workers offered him at the factory entrance where secret agents were always on the lookout.

"Good morning, Red," greeted some of his com-panions and, since Mateus walked in and out of the factory with his hat on, his red head covered, the agents gave another interpretation to that "Red" and attributed the most terrible schemes to Mateus. "The Red one" was finally called to the police station to reveal his secret association with the other Reds. Since he denied this and insisted he knew nothing about the matter, he was considered even more dangerous, even "redder" than he had appeared to be at first.

From that moment on his life became hell. No single week passed without the police coming to his house to get him. If a boiler exploded in the factory; if the son of the colonel, owner of the factory, was shot in a brothel; if there were rumors of a strike in the city, the police seemed to have no address other than the Red's to track down those responsible for the "crimes." And so that accounts for the fact that Mateus began to spend more time behind prison bars than he did in his own room on the outskirts of Jabotão. The truth is that the real Reds always considered Mateus too stupid to be trusted with any revolutionary plans. They never had anything to do with him. They never even tried to win him over to their own ideas.

All Mateus had ever learned on the subject of social justice was what he had overheard at political rallies while he was in jail. It was from behind bars that Mateus heard during a political rally that took place on the square facing the prison that it was necessary to fight to free the people from the clutches of hunger and poverty. But to fight? With what means? With weapons? The politicians who made the speeches at the rallies did not spell this out clearly, and even today Mateus, the Red, did not know how to participate in this fight.

Not being able to put up any longer with so many unjust imprisonments and questionings, one day Mateus quit his job and ended up in Afogados, where he hid among the mangroves and was among the first to build a shack in the area later to be known as Stubborn Hamlet.

The Negress Idalina also came to the marshlands to hide—not from fear, but from shame. She was ashamed before the world because of what had happened to her daughter Zefinha. Idalina was always a virtuous woman who fulfilled her duties. She had had her share of hardships in life, granted, but poverty had never prevented her from following the straight path. When her daughter, who was the object of all her devotion, took a false step in life and became a prostitute, Idalina could not stand the shame. She left her little house with a door and a window in the district of Torre and came to hide in a hovel in the midst of the mire of the marshlands.

For years the Negress Idalina had made a good living from her earnings as a cook in the homes of the rich, because she was a first-class cook, especially in the preparation of dishes from Bahia, her home. She had a good job at the house of a senator who lived in Derby when the misfortune befell her daughter. Zefinha had always been a temptation because of her beauty. She was a mulatto girl of light color and curly hair, seeming almost not to belong to her mother's race. This unexpected grace and beauty brought forth in her mother an intense and submissive love that could only be considered adoration. Idalina tried her best to keep her daughter from suffering. She did not want the girl to know hunger as she had known it, nor to have her remain illiterate like her mother, or live in a hovel, or walk barefoot like the other girls in the neighborhood. Zefinha grew up in luxury the Negress bought with her hard labor in a kitchen, always standing at a hot stove, as her father, a sugar-mill slave, had always stood by the boilers.

It was a hard life for Idalina, but her ecstatic evenings at home contemplating the beauty of her daughter, now a grown mulatto woman, curvaceous and coquettish with her fascinating white teeth and her incredibly lovely black hair, compensated for all her motherly sufferings. Zefinha's escape from home was the hardest blow in Idalina's life. When she was left alone, aware that the neighbors knew everything about her shame and that, though they showed pity in her presence, most of them took pleasure in the scandal and laughed at her in the neighborhood shops, Idalina could take it no longer. She could not bear the insult to her honor. She disappeared from the neighborhood and went to live in Stubborn Hamlet, where no one knew her and no one knew that her daughter was a fallen woman.

There Idalina lived, isolated from the world and performing with modesty her artistic cookery. She made tapioca, corn meal, and a pudding confection with grated coconut, all of which she sold on a tray at the Largo da Paz.

Soon Idalina conquered everyone in the neighborhood. She sought out no one, but when the women of the area started a conversation, she was always friendly. She was always ready to help anyone in greater need. She would help deliver a child, or nurse a very sick person, or even ease the death of people who hold on to their last breath. Idalina knew strong prayers that helped the dying cross over to the other side. Soon everyone considered Idalina a gem.

One day they brought a baby for her to bring up. It was Zefinha's son. This grandson, Oscarlindo, brought her another breath of happiness. She showed off her grandson to everyone and also spoke about his mother. She boasted of her daughter's beauty, showing a picture of the girl with a feather hat on her head and a golden bracelet on her wrist. If a listener was not familiar with the sad story of her daughter and asked why Zefinha did not live with her mother in the settlement, Idalina changed the subject. She would take a deep breath and talk about the high cost of living, while her eyes filled with tears.

Thus the Negress Idalina and the inhabitants of the hamlet lived for many years in the heavenly peace of the Lord, till one day shame lighted up anew in Idalina's heart and she left for a new hiding place, this time known to no one.

But this happened much later, and before this sad episode stirred the tranquillity of the marshlands much water had flowed down the Capibaribe, much water had passed under the bridge of Recife, and in the tumult of these waters many other adventures had taken place.

If Cosme had always been the most respected figure of Stubborn Hamlet and Idalina the best liked, Chico was doubtless the most legendary. Chico was a kind of a myth whom everyone discussed without ever seeing. All knew that he existed, though invisible, hidden in the depth of his dark hovel, the doors of which were always closed. During the day when the neighborhood swarmed with the constant come-and-go of people, no one could see Chico on the streets, or coming in and out of bars for a sip of rum. All knew that during the hours when the sun shines in the sky and men attend to their business, Chico remained curled up like an animal in his hole, hiding his leprosy. No one bothered him, no one denounced him. Chico could be at peace in his hole because he knew that no dweller of Stubborn Hamlet would make it known that there was a leper in the neighborhood, thereby causing the authorities to come for him immediately and check him into a hospital. Chico was a legend, a nocturnal apparition, almost a ghost.

Very few had seen him pass hurriedly in the late

hours of the night, taking the path to the river. The river was his great passion. Only when all life in the neighborhood had quieted down for the night, and stars and fireflies gleamed jointly above the darkness of the marshes, only then did Chico remove his raft from its constant hiding place under the clump of rushes by the edge of the river to drift on the calm waters of the Capibaribe.

Till early dawn, as the raft drifted smoothly, abandoned to the current, Chico threw his fishing net in the river and let his thoughts wander through the immensity of the night. This was his hour of happiness, the hour in which he felt penetrated to the very depths of his soul by the beauty of life, by the sweet caress of the water as it flowed through his fingers, the twinkling of the stars, and the deep silence of a sleeping world. This was the hour when Chico talked intimately with the rivers. He heard their complaints and learned to love them more and more.

On nights of full moon and high tide, when the waters reached their highest level because of the attraction of the moon, Chico steered his raft to the large river basin behind the Governor's Palace where the waters of the Capibaribe and Beberibe meet. In the midst of this enormous basin into which the moon pours a silvery cascade of light, Chico floated, attracted by the moon's magnetic force. He lost himself in the snarled history of these two rivers, a history to which the northeasterner lent, in Chico's fantasy, the impetuous and violent soul of a man born predestined to adventure.

"Para os bichos e os rios	For animals and for rivers
Nascer já é caminhar	to be born is to walk instantly
Eu não sei o que os rios	I do not know what the rivers
Têm de homens do mar."	have of men of the sea.

Lulled by the gentle currents of high tide, Chico dreamed of the impatient descent of the rivers which, with their sinuous movements, concealed their desire to meet. He thought of the Capibaribe, which came from the distant mountains of Jacararás in Cariría-Velhos and joltingly flowed over stones, passing towns and hamlets, symbolically relating all the vicissitudes of life in the backlands. Sometimes the stories were told in a humble tone. That happened during periods of drought and hardship, when the river flowed as a thin thread of water in the midst of its bed, very quietly, as if in fear of the slightest sound that might attract thirsty lips to steal its last drop. At other times its tone was boastful, and the wealth of its loud waters overran the banks, telling of the rich rains that fell in abundance. On its descent, the waters always reflected different and increasingly friendly landscapes. The hard riverbed of stones changed into a soft table of sand, and the arid landscape of the backlands, with its thorny cactuses and sharp leaves of Bromelia plants, softened to a gentler mien of a damp greenish tone and covered with thick mangroves.

The anxious waters flowed on, quite indifferent to the landscape and to the small tributaries that generously brought their waters to help the river in its descent through the lands of the northeast where everything and everyone help one another. They were humble tributaries, but each had its own story. There was the Rice Stream, and the Vulture Stream, the Cave and Crevice Streams, the Honey Stream and the Rum Stream, Wood Stream and Arara Stream, Covered Stone Stream, and God knows what other streams.

The Capibaribe moved on, deaf to these stories and blind to the regionalism of the landscape, almost overwhelmed by an infinite anxiety to meet the other famous river. Where is the Beberibe? The Beberibe has a shorter distance to go before it meets the Capibaribe. It comes from the hills of the city of Olinda.

Modest little tributaries still appear: the Camaragibe, the Monteiro, the Tegipió. But where is the Beberibe? Once in the city, the Capibaribe divides into two branches to close the Beberibe in so it cannot escape. They finally meet and embrace, and their waters mingle, submerging in profound pleasure the anxieties accumulated during long distances covered. Two famous adventurers unite contentedly, telling each other their adventures. The violence of this barbarian embrace increases their waters and, confused by the joy of their encounter, the rivers lose their sense of direction and in a drunken stagger flow over the sandbanks, then become shredded threads of water over the quagmire and rest in the coves. In this carefree manner the waters of these rivers create an anarchy of islands, channels, marshlands, and bogs, in the midst of which is set the delightful city of Recife, climax of the heroic adventures told and retold by these rivers as they meet somewhere on a beach of the Atlantic.

Late at night Chico awakened from this delightful and confused dream on the travels of the rivers and, filled with joy, directed his raft upstream on the Capibaribe. His happiness was even more intense because he knew that in a few minutes he would end his fishing trip and, as he did every night, meet his great friend Cosme.

In the turmoil of his life, Cosme had been his only anchorage. It was Cosme's kindness and patience that had saved Chico at a time when he thought of taking his raft to the high seas, never to return. It was in the refuge of Cosme's friendship that the storm abated. Only Cosme had been able to create a new interest in life within him, when he explained that there were greater pains than his, that there were uglier leprosies than his, and that he was not the only man alone in the world—that all men carry their hidden leprosy and that almost all men are alone, though one is unable to see the other's loneliness.

The splash of the lead on his fishing net as it hit the waters of the river sounded like rain falling on the roof. Chico gathered his tightly stitched net and removed half a dozen *piaba* fish. Only rarely did a larger fish show up, like a catfish, a *cioba,* or a *camorim.* What he usually got was the *piaba,* or the "tin-tin-belly" with its belly stuffed with mud.

When the first rays of the sun broke on the horizon, Chico gathered his raft and awakened Cosme to eat with him. Almost always when he arrived at his friend's hovel he found Cosme already awake, waiting for him. Cosme went to bed early. He slept with the hens, said old Totonha, his aunt, and always woke at dawn to catch the arrival of the new day in his mirror. Chico gave the fish to old Totonha. He gave her the little *piabas* to fry for their meal, and the bigger ones, when there were any, to sell at the Afogados market, so that they could get a few pennies for tobacco, rum, and flour.

They talked excitedly while the smell of fried fish made their mouths water. Cosme told secrets that he would have no courage to tell anyone else, because Cosme knew that to speak with Chico was like speaking to a tomb. No one would ever know anything he told Chico. Lately Cosme had been trying to explain to his friend that the people's situation was becoming harder every day, and that hunger was steadily increasing while the government did not make the slightest effort to improve conditions; that the politicians in power were concerned only with lining their pockets. But that all of this would end.

Cosme said he knew about the storm that the indifference of the ones in power was brewing in the land.

131

Very soon that storm would break—the fault of the landowners who did not allow the dwellers on their lands to cultivate it in order to satisfy their hunger; the fault of the factory owners who paid their workers starvation wages so that their own children might travel in luxury through Europe, as well as support concubines in lush apartments in town; and mostly, the fault of the government that saw it all—all this shamelessness of the wealthy and all the misery of the people—and yet ignored it.

Cosme's information worried Chico, because he could not see the people fighting against the power of the landowners associated with the government and protected by the police and the power of money. But Cosme told Chico he would see. People were not as stupid as they used to be. Nor as alone. They were beginning to organize their forces. The people of the northeast had loyal friends and supporters in the south, among the workers of São Paulo, the prospectors of Minas Gerais, the peasants of Rio Grande do Sul. Every night Cosme talked of the great day that was approaching for the people of the northeast.

When the first peasants started passing along the road with their baskets of fruits and vegetables for the market of Afogados, Chico took leave of his friend Cosme and rushed back to his own hovel to hide from the dangers of life and the innumerable hazards that the men who wake up after daybreak represented to him.

X

*of how
the waters
overran
the face of
the earth*

It was Juvêncio who first brought to the hamlet the threatening news. Upon returning from work early one evening, he went to the bar for a drink of rum and reported to the other patrons the rumor he had heard from the factory manager:

"It is being said that a flood is on its way; that it rained so much in the backlands that the dams are bursting; that in its descent the Capibaribe growls and foams like a snake in heat."

The description, aimed at impressing the listeners, did not create the desired effect. Manuel Palito, the owner of the bar, while calmly filling the two glasses of rum that he pushed over the counter towards Sebastião and Mateus, asked in a relaxed tone:

"Is that really true? Or is it just a stupid rumor spread by someone who has nothing else to do? If here there isn't even a sign of rain, how come there is a monster of a flood on its way?"

Juvêncio replied:

"They say that up there things are different, that in the backlands and in the arid regions it's as if the sky had dropped on the earth. That's what I've been told. Take it for what it's worth."

Still the news did not cause much alarm. The clients of the bar, dwellers of the marshlands, were used to climatic calamities, whether drought or flood, and regardless of origin in backlands or mire. They had been hardened by suffering and were experts in resisting the excesses of nature. They would not get scared just like that at vague and exaggerated rumors. Let the flood come. They would know how to brave it as they had known at other times, when the neighborhood of the marshlands, with all its houses and coconut groves, was covered by the water.

"The Deluge was even greater and Noah escaped," jokingly said Sebastião. His companions laughed, continued to drink, and picked up the conversation where Juvêncio had interrupted it. They spoke about cockfights, a subject of much greater interest than floods. Sebastião took over with enthusiasm:

"I tell you, I have still to see a gamecock capable of beating the Dourado of our friend Anastácio."

Anastácio was a retired police lieutenant who had spent many years with the rangers fighting banditry in

134

the backlands and had come to the conclusion that he agreed more with the bandits than with the police; that the bandits were much better behaved toward their families and respected them more than the soldiers did. And if Anastácio did not join the bandits, it was only because at that time he was already old and so he decided to retire and breed gamecocks in Santo Amaro. For two years this lucky man was the owner of the best gamecock in the neighborhood; some even said in the entire state. Dourado had fought and beaten in open combat the champions Caruaru and Taquaretinga which till then had been the most noted cocks of the backlands. If the fight against banditry had not brought any glory to Anastácio—to the contrary, he even felt embarrassed to admit that he had participated in that inglorious pursuit—the Dourado cock, on the other hand, had enhanced his life with resounding fame. People no longer called him Lieutenant Anastácio but Dourado's Anastácio. And he basked in this fame with undisguised satisfaction.

That day Anastácio came to the bar to inform everyone that in two days his famed cock would fight an equally famed bird from Paraíba. It was being brought from the capital of that state especially for this fight with the champion of Recife by the son of a big shot.

"That'll be a real fight," said Anastácio with modesty in his voice. "Dourado never gave a bad performance in the ring, and they say the same about the cock from

135

Paraíba, which by the way, is called Diamante. You will not be sorry that you attended the fight."

Anastácio was establishing contact with the enthusiasts of his cock, trying to win new adherents to reinforce his scanty capital and thereby enable him to watch the bets of the son of the big shot from Paraíba; also those of the crowds that would arrive by train the next day with their pockets stuffed with betting money. But Dourado's greatest admirer was right there: it was Sebastião, who acted as a kind of publicity agent and betting manager for Anastácio, and in that capacity covered all the neighborhood bars with him. It was during the performance of these duties that he would declare with conviction:

"It's our great hour approaching, men. The hour of our independence. We can become filthy rich. They say that the fellow from Paraíba is a rich man's son and is crazy about cockfighting. It is in our hands to fill our pockets with his money. All we have to do is to bet all we can on our champion. It'll be a cinch for Dourado. This so-called Diamante will beat it so fast no one will be able to catch him."

"He won't beat it, Sabastião; he'll be stretched on the ground with a broken neck, dead as a doornail," said Joca, by now all agog with the idea of this big fight next Sunday.

No one in the neighborhood showed a more consistent or enthusiastic interest in cockfighting than Joca, especially since his disabling rheumatism had definitely

136

kept him from the work of hauling sugar at the Apolo docks. The loss of this job made his life very hard.

In his youth, Joca had been a good worker. He could carry two bags of sugar at a time balanced on his head, and at table, he could eat three chickens and drink six bottles of beer at one meal. But these vaunted abilities did not endure. At thirty his strength diminished, sapped by a rheumatic pain that attacked his spine, and now, at forty, Joca was an old rag who even moved with difficulty. His bent spine and stiff neck did not allow him to really work. He lived off odd jobs such as delivering messages, giving tips on the numbers game, and habitually putting the bite on his former companions. Drinking more and more, and having less and less to eat, Joca was falling apart before everyone's eyes.

The only passion left to him was cockfighting. Whenever there was a fight, there he was at the ring with a bottle of water under his arm and a rag in his coat pocket to help restore the gasping fighters. At the height of the battle he would grab his bottle, fill his mouth with water, making his shriveled cheeks look like a balloon, and then would sprinkle the water over the angry heads of the cocks. When the head bled, the rag would clean the veil of blood covering the eyes of the fighter. Joca treated every cock with the same interest and the same enthusiasm.

To be truthful, his enthusiasm was not in the fight itself but in its final result. What really interested Joca was a perfect finish in which one of the cocks left the other stretched on the ground breathing its last through its open beak, dying right there on the field. This was what interested him. When such a finish took place, Joca enthusiastically picked up the dying cock and helped it die by discreetly twisting its featherless neck. After that he went home and feasted on chicken meat roasted on a spike.

There was a kind of tacit understanding between the owners of the cocks and Joca. Any cock killed in battle was given over to the gentle hands of Joca who during the bird's life had tended it with such thoughtful care; he had sprinkled the cock's head with water and had dried its glorious blood. Once the sacrifice was consummated, Joca felt that the battle remains were his sacred right.

Only once was this pact not respected. It was when Sem-Rival, the famed cock of Senhor Neco, who owned some dairy cattle in Madalena, died in battle under the sharp beak of Dourado. Senhor Neco thought it would be a desecration to use the body of his famed cock as food for Joca. He decided that such a glorious body should be eaten by the earth, the earth that had made it strong and valiant. He had been told that cemeteries were not only for people but that there were some for animals also, and that on the horse-breeding farm of the Lundgrens in Paulista, there was a horse—Mossoró— that had won the National Grand Prize that had a grave with a beautiful monument over it. It was the figure of a horse with two wings on his back, almost lifting him in the air for his trip to the world beyond. Senhor Neco wanted to do the same for his Sem-Rival, but without the same expense and pomp, of course. After all, a horse is a horse and a cock is a cock. Senhor Neco could not even imagine the wealth that the Lundgrens must have had to afford the construction of marble and bronze graves for their horses. But he intended to do his best. He would give Sem-Rival a decent tomb with ten inches of land in his backyard. And that was what Senhor Neco did. He snatched the dead cock from the hands of Joca, who stood there mortified by the insult, and left to fulfill his Christian duty. He tenderly dug a grave behind his house and buried his hero there, going so far as to stick a coarse wooden cross, adorned with some of the animal's tail feathers, into the soft earth that covered the battered body of Sem-Rival.

When these glorious deaths did not occur and the battle ended with the shameful escape of one of the fighters, which the owner took back to his chicken coop, Joca was helplessly left without dinner and drowned his sorrows in rum at Manuel's bar.

Today Joca was pouring down rum as an aperitif to next Sunday's great banquet, when he would eat one of the famed cocks well-roasted. This could be taken for granted. After all, these fighters were cocks of class and would not run like frightened hens chased from their nests. They would certainly resist to the very end. Dourado would do it with the prestige of the gold in his name, and Diamante with the hardness of the diamond that gave him *his* name. The fight could end only in the death of one of the heroes. And then Joca would feast on the meat, probably tough, but tasty and smelling of fame, whether Diamante's or Dourado's.

Unfortunately the big fight did not take place. Man proposes and God disposes. God opened the floodgates of heaven over the backlands and the arid lands, and the waters of the Capibaribe and its tributaries started to rise steadily. From the mountain of Jacararás deep in the interior, the waters of the Capibaribe swelled and tore down embankments, snatched fragments of earth, and covered the greenery with the red color of its muddy waters. The Vertente River, the Camaragibe, the Tegipió, all were in flood and came in fury to vomit their excessive water into the Capibaribe, but not without difficulties. The waters of this large river were by then higher than those of its tributaries, which created a great turbulence at the confluence of these vagrant rivers.

The Capibaribe and the Beberibe, the famous rivers that were normally so compatible, no longer got along in the uncontained tumult of their waters. They threw themselves at each other as if torn by a crisis of jealousy that turned them into bitter enemies. Each of them felt more justified than the other to spread out farther and to cover the whole earth. It was flood-lust. Even the more modest tributaries, such streams as the Rice, Vulture, Cave and Crevice, Honey and Rum, all invaded the fields and in their fury damaged everything, tearing down shacks, killing cattle, pulling down bridges, drowning children.

The news became more threatening daily. Even Sebastião started to relate alarming information about the flood. With his obsessive habit of seeing everything in terms of male and female conjunction, he would announce:

"They say that the rivers are covering the hinterland with the fury of stallions in heat. The Petribu River tripped the Usina and threw her in his bed. The Usina gave herself without resistance. The Mussurepe tried the same thing with his Usina, but this one, more arrogant, repulsed him and left him excited, licking his feet all night but without giving in to his desires."

The farmer Zé Baraúna, however, who came from Talhada Mountain and only thought of earth for planting, would say:

"The river is descending with a load of islands in its waters. It's a pleasure to see it. They are islands with black earth and with red earth, pieces snatched from the arid lands and from the marshlands." The poor fellow's mouth would water at the thought of how the river would lay down all that land, how it would deposit all those islands that, if sowed, would yield food to still everyone's hunger.

"They say the flood is coming this way from the marshlands of Madre de Deus where it is now. They say the village of Capado is all under water. Any time

141

now the flood will be right here in Recife," declared a stranger in the group.

The people of Stubborn Hamlet refused to believe this terrible threat. They pinned their hopes on the strong prayers capable of changing weather, and placed their trust in Providence.

"It is possible that all this uproar of the waters will become exhausted along the way and that only an echo of the flood will get to us," said Zé Luis in hope. "From the source to this shore, the river waters have a large stretch of land to cover and flood."

"But they're already nearing the shore, Zé Luis," Maria answered, worrying about her two small boys who could not swim. "A flood is a treacherous thing, man of God. You can't take chances."

But they all took chances. No one thought of moving to some other region, higher, more protected from the waters. They were fatalists and let everything take its course, having placed their lives in the hands of God. Yet, since Saturday morning, the river had been showing its growing fury. In its muddy waters floated the first bundles of green balsa, snatched from the marshes by the current, and once in a while a tree trunk would pass with its clump of leaves showing above the water. These were signs that things were getting bad. It rained all morning and the world was submerged under one solid mass of water that the wind blew down to the ground from the clouds. It was a thick rain that fell on

142

the roofs of the hovels, not in drops but in gusts, filtering through the straw and starting leaks everywhere. Soon new sounds were added to the macabre symphony of the flood. They were the metallic clinks of water falling in heavy drops into the empty tin cans placed strategically around the house to keep puddles from forming.

By the afternoon the storm was over and the sun reappeared triumphantly, and with it hope shone anew in the oppressed hearts of all those people.

"We are safe," they shouted. "The weather will change!"

And everyone went to sleep full of trust.

Idalina woke up before dawn with her back and feet ice cold. She moved in her bed and water oozed from her soaked sheets. The Negress was frightened. She struck a match and lighted the kerosene lamp that hung from the wall. The yellowish light spread phosphorescent reflections over a broad pool of muddy water. The hovel had become a little lake. The bed and stools floated like the remains of a shipwreck. A sudden terror seized Idalina:

"Could something have happened to Baé?"

Though she had not intended to speak, the question escaped her trembling lips while, with quaking legs, she jumped into the water, holding her nightgown up to her groin with one hand. She floundered in the muddy water toward the back door of the hovel, tear-

143

ing it open in her anxiety to see what had happened to her pig. Where the pigpen had stood, she found only water. There was no sign either of the pig or of the mangrove enclosure that had fenced him in.

Everything had been dragged away by the current. Idalina started to cry:

"My poor little pig . . . all that wasted effort breeding him . . . all that effort for nothing. . . ."

Her hot tears mingled with the cold water of the tide. The river growled loudly and pushed at the hovel with the fury of someone raping a woman. It licked big chunks of mud from the walls. A world was falling apart. Idalina suddenly remembered her grandson and was even more terrified. She ran back to the hovel and woke Oscarlindo, who was peacefully sleeping on his wooden cot built on a higher level than was her bed. She immediately wrung out his little clothes that lay drenched on a stool already whirling around the house. She dressed the boy in his wet clothes, put him astride her back, and left to seek help. As she stepped out of her house, Idalina anxiously warned Oscarlindo:

"Hold on tight to my back so you don't slip, Carlindo. Be careful."

The sleepy, terrified boy hardly spoke. He only sighed and moaned and clung tighter to his grandmother's back.

There was no street or road left. Water covered everything. Aside from the water, only the indifferent telephone poles and the coconut trees could be seen, swaying with the onslaughts of the current and the strong winds.

Feeling her way by the faint light of dawn and guided almost solely by instinct, Idalina sloshed toward Zé Luis' cabin. Suddenly an enormous ball hit her body and the poor woman was terrified again. It was a lace-maker's cushion carried by the tide. As it crashed against Idalina's belly, the lace bobbins snapped as if they were being moved by the competent hand of a lace-maker. Idalina thought:

"In this black hour where are the hands that moved the bobbins of this cushion? Would they still be alive, groping hands like hers, or were they now dead hands, stiff and cold, lying under the water?"

While these sad thoughts crossed Idalina's mind, the cushion passed, spinning itself into the blackness of the waters. The Negress vigorously shook her head to rout these useless thoughts and concentrated on saving her grandson who by now, shivering and drenched, weighed heavier and heavier. Idalina was trapped by the waters and saw no way out. There was not a piece of land or a boat in sight. The water continued to rise. When she had left home, the water had come up to her buttocks; now it reached her waist. Which direction to take? She decided to move toward her shack in the vague hope that a miracle had taken place, that someone had showed up at the last moment to save her and her little grandson. She walked with extreme care, moving one foot only when the toes of the other had already sunk deep into the mud. Idalina feared she would slip or stumble, thereby throwing Carlindo into the water where he would be swallowed by the torrent.

Her anguish grew steadily. Her last hopes of rescue were fading when an apparition materialized. Right in front of her and against the first rays of the sun on the horizon a strange supernatural figure appeared and, with cane in hand, walked over the waters. Before the wide-eyed Idalina and out of that background of light appeared the very image of Christ approaching over the waters as he had been seen by his disciples. And he was moving right toward her. Awed, Idalina felt a tightness in her throat and her heart beat violently. She thought of kneeling down right there, but the waters would have covered her head. Then, letting go for a moment one of Oscarlindo's thin arms, she slowly crossed herself with her wet hand. Her eyes dimmed by tears, she waited for the figure to approach. As it came closer, the apparition took more definite shape. It was Chico, the leper, his pants and shirt in shreds, drifting on his raft that the rebellious waters had covered. He held a long boat hook in his hands and with it fought the current to keep the raft away from the reefs. Idalina was unable to speak. She merely smiled a blissful smile, which floated on her tearful face.

Chico placed the old woman and her grandson on his raft. He explained that he had come just to save them. It was his third trip since he had left home. He had saved Cosme and his aunt, Zé Luis and his family, and he had already passed by Idalina's hovel and found it empty. At that point Chico's explanation caught Oscarlindo's interest. He felt better now and asked where João Paulo was. Chico informed him that the boy was safe in the fort of Buraco to which they were heading.

When Idalina recovered her voice, she asked Chico who had informed him in time that the flood was approaching. Chico smiled with his thick and deformed lips and laconically replied:

"It was the river who informed me."

And it was true. The river held no secrets from Chico. For years they had been conversing, and he had long since discovered the complete meaning of the language of the river as it talked with the marshlands, the rafts, and the fishermen.

On the eve of the flood Chico had gone fishing but, as he reached the river's edge, he felt he was passing something strange. The river gently licked the higher branches of the mangroves as a cow licks the head of its calf while mooing softly. Chico listened closely to understand the meaning of that mooing of the waters. And he understood it as a flood warning. It was the river caressing the marshlands and warning them of the danger about to come, so they would hold on tight with their branches and roots to withstand the flood's violence. Chico could not misunderstand this warning. He pulled his raft to a higher place, tying it well on the trunk of a coconut tree, and then went to inform Cosme of what the river had told him. They agreed about where to go to be saved from the flood. Neither Chico nor Cosme wanted to be among too many people, therefore it would not be wise for them to go up to the hill of Olinda, or that of Prazeres, or that of Chapéu, which would most probably be crowded with all the people who would come out of the mire when the waters of the river had covered it with the flood.

They decided to go to the old Fortress of Buraco, an ancient fort built three centuries ago by the Dutch, on the end of the isthmus of Olinda, abandoned today to the crabs and sea gulls, between the river and the sea. They would remain there sheltered and isolated until the waters lowered. And that was what they did. Before the waters went high enough to threaten Cosme's hovel, Chico took his raft upstream toward the entrance to his friend's shack. Helped by old Ana, he carried the paralytic in his arms to the raft. It did not demand too much effort because Cosme weighed less than a child. Aside from his head, everything was thin and dry. Wrapped in a sheet, he was more like a bunch of dry twigs than a creature.

When, after this last trip with Idalina and her grandson, Chico arrived at the fortress, there were more people there than he had expected to find. It was because several dwellers of the district of Santo Amaro had come on improvised rafts built with mangrove logs, rafters, and old boards, drifting to the isthmus of Olinda, from whence they walked to the fortress.

Juvêncio and Senhor Maneca were among these peo-

148

ple, and they helped Idalina climb the steep breakwaters of the fortress. Juvêncio complained constantly about the catastrophe, particularly that the flood had invaded his hovel and snatched from his floor the tiles that represented so much time and effort. He lamented the wasted months of work and all those days when he had carried the tiles one by one in his shirt, the cold of the stone giving him goose flesh—all that just to cover the dirty depths of the river. During the rest of the day Idalina and Juvêncio competed for the compassion of their listeners over their dark misery. Idalina wept over the loss of her pig and Juvêncio mourned his tiles.

It was already broad daylight and the sun struck sparks about the mire when Chico again left the fort on his raft to continue rescuing people. By that time there were several better-equipped boats charged with the task. They were motor boats of the Maritime Police, gathering shipwrecked people perched on the ridgepoles of their houses, holding on tightly to the crowns of the coconut trees, or squatting on the piles of stones placed here and there for road construction, which the current threatened to demolish. Several canoes went downstream jammed with people and animals: goats, dogs, chickens, parrots, and caged birds in an assortment reminiscent of Noah's Ark.

The current was becoming stronger and so Chico thought it wise to return to the fort, find a dark corner for himself, and rest.

João Paulo and Oscarlindo, leaning over the railing

of the fort, watched as if from a grandstand the fiesta of the waters. They followed the descent of the trees and balsa that sprinkled the red of the flood with green.

Many dead animals went by, sheep, dogs, and goats. Even cows floated by with enormous stomachs distended by gases, their heads submerged, appearing to be more whale than cow. The vultures mounted the carcasses and traveled downstream clinging to the carrion. Occasionally dead chickens passed by and the crews of the barges and rafts tried to catch them in order to have some food for the hard days ahead.

The growling of the waters became louder as the volume swelled along with the force of the current. Every now and then an overturned boat discharged its human load which struggled wildly to find refuge on other boats, logs, or anything still afloat in the whirlpool of the waters.

By the afternoon the sea, the rivers, and the valleys were all one mass of waters, a huge red sea extending from Fundão to the lighthouse of Barra. The marshlands, the plantations, the vegetable gardens, and the hovels were all under water. Even the mills of Várzea disappeared and only their chimneys remained visible, as if they were darkened lighthouses in a sea of despair.

The river had no respect for rank or wealth. It even started to invade the wealthy districts, with their houses of brick and tile. In the district of Madalena, all those small palaces, built on top of high stone ramparts where the river curves, were also flooded.

The servants ran panting, and carried fine carpets, valuable furniture, china, and crystal to the upper floors. Housewives knelt with their daughters and prayed before open sanctuaries. The smell of burning candles mixed with the odor of mud that came on the tide.

The church of Afogados, built on a hilltop, was filled with people. They all came in search of a piece of earth on which to stand, and in search of comfort and support. They clung to the saints, and to the words of Father Aristides. The priest opened the doors of the church, lighted the candles, and ordered Veremundo to serve coffee and cornbread to the needier in the sacristy. He asked the people to have faith in God.

At night the still-mounting waters reached the church portals. The people entered the temple and settled down with their backs against the walls, resting their worn-out bodies. The first colds showed up. An uninterrupted chorus of coughs went up the aisle of the church and prevented everyone from sleeping. So did the roaring waters outside, and the growling stomachs, and the humming of mosquitoes buzzing the whole night through.

When the day came the boys caught many crabs from the portals of the church. There were even *chiés,* those small crabs with legs disproportionately large for their diminutive bodies. The *chiés* climbed the walls like lizards.

The government motor boats now brought water

and provisions to the isolated groups. They distributed coffee, sugar, cornbread, and a mixture of cooked beans with manioc carried in large wooden vats. When one of these boats stopped before a crowd of people, hands stretched out, swaying impatiently at the end of emaciated arms—the provisions were hardly ever enough to satisfy the sea of anguished hands and famished mouths.

In the early evening a boat anchored at the ramparts of the church of Afogados and from it, tumbling and pushed by the rescue patrol, three Homeric figures appeared: Manuel Palito, Joca, and Sebastião. All three were drunk and leaned on one another for support. That was because Manuel Palito had refused to leave his rum bottles. Since he could not save them, he decided to risk his life by staying. He sat on the high counter of his tavern and remained there waiting to see what would happen. Sebastião and Joca felt sympathetic toward Manuel's cause and decided to join him in the resistance. So the three spent the whole day drinking rum and occasionally chewing a piece of cornbread. They stayed there until the rescue patrol floated by in their boat and sighted them. Then the resistance movement caved in. As the three heroes arrived at the front yard of the church, the bells tolled the Ave Maria and Father Aristides started a sermon to console his flock of helpless sheep. The priest said patience was the greatest of all virtues. He evoked the figure of Job, who so often had suffered so much more than had the flood victims and yet accepted it all with resignation. He spoke about divine wisdom and eternal justice. If today they suffered the affliction of the flood, it was doubtless because they deserved it. Let each one examine his conscience. Let everyone make penance for all the sins committed. Did they remember to come to mass on Sundays? Very few! The majority would be more apt to be present at the bars or at the cock fights. What did they expect?

At this point in the sermon, Joca exploded. He began to complain and curse in the back of the church. In Joca's confused spirit this divine justice that distributed suffering so unevenly seemed strange. If it did not rain and there was a drought, it was the poor who died of hunger. If it rained too much and there was a flood, again it was the poor whose houses were flooded and destroyed.

"Why doesn't the deluge come to drown once and for all the depraved wealthy who live in an eternal spree, do no work, and feed on abusing the wretched? What kind of divine justice is it that ignores this exploitation and closes its eyes to the dark misery of the poor!"

Just consider his own case! Joca had always worked like a madman, he had never harmed a mosquito, and his reward had been a deforming rheumatism. And that week, when the preparations were being made for the great cock fight of the coming Sunday, his hobby and the only consolation that afforded him the possibility of eating a piece of meat, this damn flood had to come and prevent the fight from taking place, taking the bread from his mouth. This was not right! It wasn't fair!

The others tried to calm Joca, but he continued to growl, brandishing the bottle of rum he had saved from the merciless flood waters.

Next day the waters gradually started to subside. The current was still strong, but it allowed an aquatic procession to take place without any danger on the Beberibe, which was calmer than the Capibaribe. A large canoe went downstream from Feitosa. It was jammed with singing women, one of them holding high in her arms an image of Saint Anthony. On the bow of the ship, named *Morning Star,* were many flowers sticky with mire, and lighted candles that occasionally were put out by the wind. The litanies went into the air and were spread by the wind through the vastness of the waters. Along the bank of the river other candles were lighted and stuck in the mud. Here and there the chanting of litanies was answered by voices singing Xangô, thus mixing Saint Anthony with the saints of African magic. Pressured by all these prayers, all this strong mixture of miraculous ritual, the waters weakened in their violence and obediently started to ebb. A dark stripe, as straight as the hem of a skirt and steadily growing larger, appeared on the façades of the houses and the higher walls. It was the sign of the lowering waters.

There was much hunger and much confusion. Many people had disappeared. Worried mothers called their young daughters, who were hidden in the holes, lost in the embrace of local lads, and gave no sign of life.

"Maroca! Júlia! Severina. . . ."

The distressed calls crossed the river from both sides and remained unanswered.

"You little hussy, taking advantage of the flood to fool around God knows where!"

Suffering was great, but hope was reappearing. And so was impatience for the waters to lower faster and for organized life to begin anew, for houses to be rebuilt and for families to be reunited, for crabs to be caught; for growing and multiplying.

XI

of how the receding flood waters dragged with them the marsh dwellers' remaining will to live . . .

When the tide runs high, the waters invade the earth with the violence of passion. When its possessive rage is drained and the waters lower, all the damage of the furious passion comes into view. All its work of destruction is engraved on the skin of the earth and on the skin of people too.

One week after the great tide, mud was already in sight. Its rotten smell rose in the air as strong as ever and mixed with the smell of carrion grounded by the receding tide and barely covered by black sheets of mud. Only the mangroves emerged triumphantly from amid this bleakness—the lush mangroves with their shining green leaves polished like metal. The mangroves reappeared as fresh as ever, as if they had just made love. Perhaps that was the secret of their lushness.

Chico declared with an expert air that while they remain under water, the mangroves devote all their time to making love; to abandoning their leaves to the impetuous kisses of the current; to rubbing their branches together with infinite voluptuousness; to sinking their thick roots pleasurably in the soft mud at the river bottom. Chico declared that on certain nights he had even heard the nuptial dance of the mangroves in the depth of the waters, and the cracking of their vigorous stalks in the slimy flesh of the mire. It was a violent transport of love that ended in a final orgasm, pouring the mangrove seed into the high waters of the tide to fertilize the new lands that would emerge from the womb of the waters.

If the nuptial dances and amorous lust of the mangroves during times of spate are facts hard to prove and perhaps existed only in Chico's sick mind, the delivery of new islands is a definite fact, in which neither imagination nor fantasy participate. Flood always improvises new geography. It makes lands appear in one spot and disappear in another. The new lands born from the womb of the waters appear at first as small miry crowns that the marshland vegetation soon covers gently to make them grow and settle.

But not only the islands swelled after the descent of the waters. The bellies of single girls grew—all those silly girls who had disobeyed their mothers' advice and carelessly satisfied their repressed instincts, sleeping among mangroves and under the caressing shade of coconut palms with dark mulattoes excited by the fury of the flood.

That was what happened to Zita and Clotilde, who for so many years had resisted the advances of slick city fellows but were unable to resist the impetuousness of the flood.

Nine months after the flood the earth gathered its good harvest of children of the marshlands; fatherless children, children without means or future, condemned to grub in the marshlands and from the mire extract their sustenance, the meat and broth of crab. And like crabs, to grow while following the movements of the tides.

The flood delivered islands, the girls delivered children, but no one was happy with so much land and so many people to baptize. Far from it. What existed was a pervading melancholy. The people came out of the flood discouraged, their heads lowered like the withered crest of a beaten cock chased from the ring.

It was as if the waters, when they ebbed, had carried with them all the energy of the flood victims, all the heroic force that they had utilized so well during the calamity, force that had seemed inexhaustible but that suddenly disappeared once the tide lowered. For with the descent of the waters, the lives of the inhabitants of the marshlands, far from improving, became steadily worse. Hunger increased. As soon as the acute phase of the catastrophe was over, the public powers suspended the help extended till then to the victims. It is true that the federal government had approved a large grant to help the flood victims. But the local politicians decided they had given enough help and that now they deserved to be rewarded for the huge sacrifices they had made. Thus it was that, as the waters of the tide meekly ran down to the sea, the money from the federal grants skillfully poured into the capacious pockets of the politicians and landowners. The victims never even saw the color of this money.

Their situation became steadily more desperate. With the terrible damage caused by the flood to the plantations of the farming region of the Zona-da-Mata, the price of food rose frighteningly, and crabbing was much more difficult in this deluge of mire that seemed to cover the world.

It is true that during high tide crabbing did not take place. But then, other fishing did. Dead animals brought by the current were caught. There were families that during the flood had feasted on flavorful entrails prepared from pieces of dead sheep carried by the waters. Now there were no animals left, dead or alive. There were only men, half dead with hunger and not knowing what to do.

Hunger spread mercilessly and joined with diseases that frighteningly proliferated with the flood. Malaria struck down half the people and their teeth chattered with tertian fever. Grippe, pleurisy, pneumonia spared no one. Tuberculosis came galloping. No family was without a sick member under its roof.

Dark misery had settled in the marshlands, making conditions ripe for revolt. This misery was so stark and menacing that the residents of wealthy neighborhoods felt compassionate and decided to do something in order to help the flood victims. The ladies of high society resolved to help those poor people by organizing a charity dance for their benefit. Since Carnival was approaching, they determined to make it a masked ball at the Jockey Club. From the invoices of this memorable ball, which took place at the headquarters of the club at the Avenida Conde de Boa Vista, a few details are worthy of mention: an unusual consumption of bottles of champagne, an also sizeable consumption of cases of whisky, the sale by auction of several gifts graciously donated by the larger firms, and the obvious demonstration by the business people of their concern for the fate of the poor. One should not forget, too, the cash balance that remained once the expenses of decoration, lighting, and service had been settled. This amount was wholly applied to the purchase of medicines, clothes, and food for the victims of the flood—to be more precise, for the children of those flood victims who had maintained good relations with the aristocratic families of the city.

Unfortunately, an affair like that cannot take place every day, and by the following day, the effects of the help had evaporated like one drop of water in a sea of misery. It was easy for those "ungrateful people" to quickly forget the favors received. The more the waters of the flood subsided, the more the people's bitter anger grew against their "benefactors," the wealthy classes who had "helped" so much during the tragedy. Such is the world.

Although weak, famished, and run down, the marshland people began the reconstruction of their shacks. This time there was no police intervention preventing their work. It seems that the drama of the flood had touched the feelings of even the public authorities who softened their customary attitudes during this time of such suffering and natural disaster. They even tried to help. Januário appeared in the neighborhood. He had recently been elected local magistrate of the area. He offered help in the form of material for the construction of houses to all dwellers who could read and write on condition that they present themselves during the week at the headquarters of the government's party to take out a voter's registration card, or renew the old one for the coming elections. Inexplicably, Zé Luis, who could read and write, flatly refused the offer. When the offended Januário asked him why he refused it, Zé Luis answered enigmatically:

"Because I rule over my hunger."

Try to understand these people, bogged down in their own misery, undergoing every imaginable hardship, who still allow themselves the luxury of refusing the government's help!

This is because the people of the marshlands, especially the ones who came down from the backlands during the drought, chased by hunger and thirst were, as a rule, tough. It was hard for them to adapt to the rules of city life. They were rebellious, rough, stiff-necked. The behavior of these people reminds one of the rush, a plant that also lives in the marshes.

The rush resists the strongest winds; the more it is forced to bend, the more it straightens up. Such were the backlanders, even when bogged down in the mire. It is not that they were arrogant; they were even humble. They endured their hardships with resignation, their heads lowered before important people. But do not ask them to lower their heads too much or they would bare their teeth.

They were not made for bootlicking. They would not vote for a government that starved them to death—a government associated with big landowners who had mercilessly expelled them from their lands; who sent their bullies to uproot the poor people's small manioc and bean gardens, which they had planted on their holidays, because those big shots did not want their own noble and green cane plantations to be soiled by the stains of these small gardens of the poor; a government of moneybags who filled their bellies with grants designed to improve the lot of the flood victims. That was the meaning of Zé Luis's sentence: "I rule over my own hunger."

They preferred to continue starving to death rather

than sell their dignity cheaply. Let the government give alms to the crippled, not to those who could, and would work.

The humiliating charity, the sending of pills and fortifying tonics for people who needed food—beans and flour to kill their chronic hunger—exasperated them more than actual indifference.

It would have been better for the government if it had continued to exist together with the upper classes, at a good distance from these poor people; and if it had also continued to ignore their misery. It would have been better than this pretense of wanting to fight their hunger with several bottles of tonic and with masked balls to purchase medication.

The flood brought forth the bitterness of these people. Now that the waters had lowered, that bitterness over life spread all over and contaminated everything. They no longer built their houses as before, with music and singing, but in the oppressive silence of people condemned to death. No more *maracatus* or *bumba-meu-bois*. There was only sadness and bleakness. Only Joca, with his mind always burning in rum, was able to maintain good humor in the midst of general sadness. When he entered the bar of Manuel Palito to drink his rum and kill time, the solicitous proprietor asked him:

"How's life, Joca?"

"I am playing the flute, old friend." [Enjoying life.]

The answer surprised everyone. First, because this

was no time for "playing the flute." Second, because everyone present at the bar was acquainted with the hardships in Joca's life, with all his needs, and how he was up to his neck in debt. How could he now say that he lived playing the flute? Joca read the surprise in the eyes of his listeners and explained with a mocking air:

"But that's how it is, my friend. If I continually borrow from one to pay the other, it's like opening a hole to close another one; just like playing the flute. . . ."

His audience now understood him better and laughed uneasily at his bleak humor. There was no more true joy, there were no more parties in the marshlands. Instead, they had secret meetings for the organization of a liberating revolution, one that would overthrow this government of crooks.

The meetings generally took place at Cosme's hovel. Cosme was still the true leader of these people, in spite of further damage to his poor body wrought by the flood. Cosme had changed considerably after the flood. It seemed now that his physical paralysis extended to his spirit. He was no longer that human volcano spewing flame from his imposing head. The volcano was slowly being extinguished. Sometimes Cosme spent long hours in a day, his little mirror abandoned next to his bed, all contacts with the world cut off. He was overcome by the darkness of his misfortune. No one knew if it was the chill he caught during those tormenting voyages when he lay over the wet wood of the raft during the days of the flood or the sight of so much suffering that drained his remaining strength.

He became thinner than ever, but still he fought for life and applied the shred of his strength to help his companions free themselves of their misery.

Men came from all over to confer with Cosme and exchange ideas with the head of Stubborn Hamlet—the leaders of the harbor workers, of the government employees, and the street-car lines. All came. From greater distances came peasant leaders who brought complaints about their life in the sugar mills and told of their revolt caused by what they suffered from the sugar-mill owners. They related that after the flood had destroyed several cane plantations, the owners had become really cruel and had increased their persecution against the small farmers, threatening to chase them from their lands for any stupid reason and refusing to pay salaries. The small landowners were forced to replant ruined cane plantations in return only for food because there was no money. They worked for a few beans and some flour and rum and molasses to prepare their *garapa* refreshment made of cane and lemon juice. If they would not work for this price, they were told to go to hell. And they were cautioned to be silent because if they talked, if they dared to claim the improvements they had made to their boss's lands—the straw hut, the kale fields, and the pigsty—the bullies would come and lower the boom on their rumps. And let that be a lesson to everyone. Damn the flood and damn the political organization that so oppressed the miserable life of the defenseless peasants.

Cosme called some of the more responsible men of Stubborn Hamlet to participate in these political meetings. He called them with his little hand-mirror, making secret signs on their faces as they walked to work, telling them the day of the meeting. That night they would all be there in his hovel. Not one was ever missing; they were all obedient to the orders of their chief.

João Paulo always attended these meetings. He came with his father. He sat in one corner of the shack with his eyes on the faces of the speakers who told of their tragic problems. One day someone showed up at the meeting who deeply impressed João Paulo. It was Nascimento-o-Grande, professional scuffler. The boy had heard of his fame. He was a tough man and, according to what was said, was responsible for many a killing. However, he had always killed face to face with the victim, wielding his fish knife in an honest fight with his adversary. His fights were generally caused by jealousy. Nascimento-o-Grande supported several colored country girls in different districts of Recife. Each night he slept at the house of a different one. Sometimes he changed the program at the last minute and showed up where he was not expected, and the night of love became instead one of blood; the blood of the unfaithful girl mixed with that of the mulatto whose path had unwisely crossed that of Nascimento-o-Grande.

He arrived quietly at Cosme's hovel. His step was

light, and he came swinging like a wildcat with his almost six-foot body. He took off his wide-brimmed hat and with a smile on his lips greeted everyone. João Paulo was in rapture before that imposing figure and the fact that this man, who was so brave though ill-famed, came to Cosme's hut to hear the voice of his friend. It was something for João Paulo to be proud of.

No important decisions would come out of these meetings. These were made on a higher level. At Cosme's house, only the manner in which the battle should be fought in the area of the hovels was discussed, as well as how to use the mire of the marshes as battle trenches.

The well-informed men brought news that soon the necessary weapons would arrive from the south and then the date of the uprising could be set. Let Cosme prepare his men and report how many fingers could be counted to pull triggers.

Cosme added up his figures inwardly and remained silent.

XII

of the
fate of the poor
of the Northeast:
to die and learn . . .

Idalina was already resigned to the loss of her pig and had resumed her normal life of selling coconut tapioca and confections of corn meal at the market of Afogados and eating her sparse beans with crabmeat, when fate played another trick on her. It was on a very bright and cheerful Sunday that Stubborn Hamlet lost its Negress Idalina.

In the vacant lot on which popular performances were held, there was a singers' competition. The neighborhood people attentively followed the two guitar players who played and sang. A crowd of people surrounded the singers; some stood, others squatted on the ground, others sat on kerosene cases. When Idalina appeared with her portable iron stove on her head and her bowl with manioc and coconut to make tapioca under her arm, Sebastião, who by then had had his fill of rum, jumped up from the circle of the singers and, running around the Negress, yelled:

"Idalina's daughter is a tramp! She is the best woman on Rua do Fogo! I slept with her yesterday on Rua do Fogo!"

The lunatic had not yet finished screaming when Idalina's stove lowered violently on his head, smashing his face completely. Sebastião fell in a puddle of blood surrounded by embers from the stove. At the same moment two soldiers who were listening to the romantic songs of the guitar players arrested the Negress.

Everyone was struck dumb by the brutality of the scene. Idalina had always been so gentle, so humble, and now, all of a sudden. . . . No one knew what to do. The truth is that few liked Sebastião, who was always rude, ill-mannered, and remiss in his behavior. It was quite true that he was talented. With his hands and a sharp knife he could carve in coconut shells charming images and figures. But he did not live from his art because he was lazy.

His life was somewhat obscure. One day he had even been caught stealing from the box for the souls in purgatory in the church of Afogados. Everyone knew the story. Every week when Father Aristides opened the box for alms he would find it empty, and yet the sacristan swore he had seen the penitents putting their alms in it during the entire week. It was a mystery. Sacristan Veremundo decided to remain on secret watch in the church to catch the thief, and he did. Late one afternoon, at the time of the Ave Maria, the sacristan saw Sebastião quietly enter the church with a bundle of sugar-cane husks under his arm. Stopping next to the box for alms, which stood behind a pillar, the thief stuck a stalk of cane husk through the opening of the box and then withdrew it with a coin attached to its end.

At first the sacristan did not understand the mystery. How was it that the cane husk attracted the coin? He ran in search of Father Aristides and the two caught Sebastião in the act of stealing from the box for souls. The mystery was easy to solve. Sebastião rubbed the juice of a very viscous fruit, the *jaca,* on the edge of the stalk he fashioned from the cane peel, and the glue caught the coins on the bottom of the box, which was soon emptied. The priest did not want Sebastião to be put in jail. He just gave him a lecture. But the sacristan spread the story and Sebastião's popularity in the neighborhood dropped considerably. That was why today, in the scene with the Negress Idalina, all sympathies were on her side. But no one dared say a word in protest against the police orders.

Escorted by the two soldiers and again with her humble appearance, Idalina started to walk away. She did not take leave of anyone. She lifted her eyes to no one. And as she walked, tears fell from her eyes to the warm sand of the street, and all the tragedies she had suffered because of her daughter's disgrace passed through her tired mind. She remembered the doctor who had seduced Zefinha. He had graduated in Bahia and had come to serve at the health center of Torre.

She remembered how he gave Zefinha samples of syrups for her cough. Then the series of injections, and Zefinha's escape after the thirteenth. The center had remained abandoned, without a doctor for several days. Then her daughter returned with swollen eyes, red from much crying. Idalina was helpless but she thanked God for letting her see her daughter again and cursed her fate for the shame she had to endure. Later, her daughter ran away again when her doctor, who had been transferred to Garanhuns, called her. Then came sad letters, saying that the man was a real no-good and that he had thrown her out on the street and abandoned her there.

The girl would not come home for the second time, but would instead pay a high price for her madness. A more comforting letter came. She had found a gentler man, a middle-aged civil servant. More confusion. The man was married and his family suddenly had arrived from another state. From then on, so as not to die of hunger, Zefinha passed from hand to hand. A traveling salesman, a pharmacist's assistant, a truck driver, and finally a hazy anonymous crowd of people—men she had no time to choose or get to know. She returned to the capital and went to live in the district of São José. Then, on a second floor of the Rua do Rosário, and finally at the Rua do Fogo. Steadily going down the ladder, there was her Zefinha now, living in a house with green windows on the Rua do Fogo, the same street where years ago a German sailor, while passing through Recife, gave another little mulatto girl a red-haired son, Mateus.

With her head still bent, Idalina crossed the bridge of Afogados, where urchins crabbed *sirís*. They were startled to see her between two soldiers. Her memories insistently whirling in her head, Idalina had no time to think about her crime before she arrived at the police station. She was immediately questioned by the chief. But, since she would only sob quietly instead of answering the questions put to her, the authority ordered one of the soldiers to relate the case. He did so quite naturally:

"Sebastião, a fellow from the hamlet, said that her daughter was a whore at Rua do Fogo and she smashed his whole face with an iron stove."

Turning to Idalina, the chief asked:

"Is it a lie that your daughter lives on Rua do Fogo?"

This time Idalina answered:

"No sir, it's true."

"And why did you want to kill the man if he was telling the truth?"

"Because not every truth should be spoken out in the open," answered Idalina with a voice much steadier and no longer shaken by sobs. Again she lowered her eyes.

The chief closed the questioning, and for the sake of justice, compassion, or prudence—who knows the real motives for human actions?—ordered Idalina to be set free and allowed to return home in peace.

But she did not return. Through a carrier, she had her grandson and her sparse household effects brought to her and never again did she set foot in Stubborn Hamlet. No one ever heard of the whereabouts of the Negress Idalina.

A few days later the hamlet lost Cosme. Chico was sleeping peacefully in his bed, when someone knocked at the door. Chico became frightened. Who would dare to look for him in his hovel in broad daylight? Would it be the police? Perhaps the health inspectors had come to take him by force? Carefully he opened the door and saw that it was João Paulo. The boy, in a troubled voice, explained that old Totonha had asked him to call Chico immediately, as Cosme had fainted. Chico ran all the way. It was the first time he appeared along the streets of Stubborn Hamlet in broad daylight. He stumbled on the lumps of the irregular road, his eyes half closed and blinded by the sun he was not accustomed to seeing. Old Totonha explained in a low voice that Cosme had fainted three times that day. The first time was unexpected, and at that moment his little mirror fell from his hand and broke into pieces. Then Cosme regained consciousness. But the last two times he took a lot longer to recover, and she was frightened that the next time Cosme would go once and for all.

Other people were already in the shack. Zé Luis advised them to call a doctor. But Cosme shook his head no. He wanted to die peacefully, as peacefully as he had lived in his corner. They respected his wish. For two days and one night Cosme hovered between life and death. They called no doctor, but instead Maria das Dores came. She was the one who, after Idalina's departure, eased the dying in the neighborhood. While old Totonha wept and Maria das Dores prayed, Chico and João Paulo did not take their eyes off Cosme.

The entire neighborhood learned of Cosme's nearing death and a huge pilgrimage was made to his hovel. All day long people came and talked under the coconut trees, lamenting the event.

Right now, when they were particularly in need of Cosme's advice and experience, death had impatiently come to claim him; now, when the decisive hour for everyone's liberty was approaching. Cosme himself had informed them that the date of the uprising had been set. It would be soon.

"He is the only one who can lead our battle," someone said.

"Without Cosme we are lost, as if we had no head, like a crab in a storm," replied another in a troubled voice.

The distress was general. Now and then Cosme, in his death agony, would come out of his stupor and utter short, gentle sentences to his friends. But he no longer spoke of the Revolution.

On the second night he gave a deep sigh and fainted away as if he had completely lost his breath. Das Dores said that the moment had come and asked for a candle to put in the hand of the dying man. There was no candle in the house, nor in any of the huts of the neighbors who were present. They were all very poor people. So Das Dores took a piece of burning twig from the fire and placed it carefully between Cosme's hands. This way, he would depart to the darkness of the other world with the light from the wood showing him the way. But the moment of departure had not yet arrived. Once more Cosme regained consciousness and saw the burning twig in his hands, which were folded over his chest. He understood what was taking place and said in a deep and slow voice:

"Die and learn."

Those were his last words. Moments later, Cosme died.

XIII

*of how
João Paulo, as he
heard the storm created
by men, turned into
a crab . . .*

João Paulo was no longer the same. He was changed.
He no longer breathed the breath of life with the eager-
ness of by-gone days. With the death of his friend
Cosme and the unexpected departure of the Negress
Idalina with Oscarlindo, his companion in fun, the
hamlet held little attraction for him. The marshes now
seemed to him to be nothing but a thick miry blob of
mud offering nothing. His eyes no longer saw happy
colors in the landscape. Only somber colors drifted in
his heart.

João Paulo even lost interest in games. He no longer
felt like flying a kite by the edge of the river, or playing
ball with other boys his own age, or hooking a ride on
the streetcar from Pina to the city to see the streets
jammed with automobiles and the store windows filled
with strange objects, rich clothing, and beautiful things

manufactured in a world apart and distant from his own. All these were matters of indifference to him now. When there was no work for him, João Paulo would remain in bed motionless, his eyes fixed on the ceiling of the hovel. And he would think. He thought only of the sad things that were the substance of his people: the emptiness of life, poverty, death.

This alienation, and João Paulo's long silences, worried his mother. She told Zé Luis of the strange behavior of their son, of his constant moodiness and isolation that made him look like an old man with no more interest in life. Zé Luis started to observe his son closely and also began to worry. He had never seen the boy with such a serious and thoughtful expression on his face, as if he had tormenting problems on his mind. He decided to bring into the open the causes for that change.

This morning, while they ate their customary meal—crabs and watered-down coffee—Zé Luis questioned João Paulo. He wanted to know why his son was not happy. Perhaps he no longer enjoyed working for the parish priest?

The son found it difficult to explain what he felt, but he assured Zé Luis that it was not that, that he even liked the priest very much and enjoyed crabbing *guaiamus* with him. Clumsily putting his words together, without finding ways to express himself clearly, João Paulo said that he was sad to see so much poverty and suffering in the world and to be unable to help. His father, almost in a tone of reproach, told him that this was none of his business. It was not for him to think about this sad nonsense, that this was not a subject for children but a problem for grownups. João Paulo kept quiet and the conversation died away.

After the meal João Paulo left for the house of the parish priest. He walked slowly but steadily, and his head was bent forward, as if his thoughts weighed too much for him to keep his head straight over his thin neck. His eyes were fixed on the ground, as if the world around him no longer deserved being seen.

João Paulo was walking in the lonely silence when suddenly he heard a series of strange noises that made him shiver. They sounded like claps of thunder resounding nearby, followed by wind whistling between the leaves of trees. It was probably a storm, he thought. João Paulo looked at the sky. It was clear and held no clouds. This was a strange storm, with no clouds and no sign of rain, but with a shining sun in the blue sky. He got scared. The storm continued. The thunderclaps echoed all over, strangely, as if cut into small pieces that rattled in a frightening rhythm.

João Paulo stood still, trying to decide from which side these strange thundering noises came. They seemed to come from all corners: sometimes from the city, sometimes from Afogados, sometimes from the Beberibe, sometimes from the other side of the marshes. João Paulo felt a turmoil in his head and shivers running through his body. He started to run, zigzag, as do the crabs, trying to decide where the thunderclaps came from.

As he ran, he saw that the hovel dwellers had all come to the doors and were looking at the sky with terror on their faces. João Paulo kept running. He heard his name called twice but gave no heed. Nothing interested him there any more. All he cared about was to discover where the storm was. He took shortcuts, crossed footbridges, ran through vacant lots, and when he reached the foot of the bridge of Afogados, he faced the storm. From the riverbank he saw, squatting down by the marshes, several men armed with rifles and machine guns, firing furiously. The machine guns explained the rattling thunderclaps and the bullets whistled like a death wind through the fat leaves of the mangroves.

João Paulo descended the riverbank and mingled with the men. He knew no one personally, but felt that they all belonged to that family he admired so much: the family of the heroes of the marsh. Many of them were almost naked, as if they were crabbing in the marshes, and their bodies were covered only with large mud stains. They were the same knights of misery who had lived through so many heroic battles in João Paulo's overactive imagination. Today these knights of misery were protected not only by their muddy armor but also by weapons—rifles and machine guns—which no one knew where they had acquired. Only Cosme would know and explain it all to him. But Cosme was dead. And anyway, there would be no time to ask questions now.

The storm these men were creating was no game. It was not like the storms he, João Paulo, fabricated with Father Aristides for the capture of *guaiamus*. Running from one end to the other, the boy started to help load machine guns while the men aimed their weapons at the yellow spots of soldiers' uniforms, which got confused sometimes with the yellowish leaves of the marsh on the other bank of the river. When the live stains disappeared from within the tree leaves, the men would pause in their shooting and then the same stormy noises could be heard coming from other areas of the city.

The turmoil in Stubborn Hamlet was great. Men ran from one spot to another, not knowing what to do. Even Chico appeared at the door of his hovel. He joined the others, exclaiming:

"The revolution is here! Cosme was right when he said that we were on the eve of the revolution!"

The men questioned one another, but no one was able to explain anything. No one knew anything. Not one of them was a part of the machinery of the revolution, though they were all rebels.

In the city, there was panic. Tradesmen hurriedly closed the doors of their shops, women ran home like madwomen, battalions of the Military Police marched quickly toward strategic points in order to smother the revolution. In the cafés of the center, certain individuals who considered themselves well informed declared that it was nothing but the uprising of a battalion instigated by its sergeants and linked up with workers and peasants who were willing to die to end hunger. Others said it was more serious than that, that the uprising was a part of other movements around the country, and that soon rebel warships would appear in the harbor and bomb the palace of the governor. There was great expectation.

All day long the noise of weapons rattled but no one knew for sure what was happening.

In Stubborn Hamlet the views were divided.

Joca was optimistic:

"It's all right. This lousy government is going to the ground."

He recalled that it would not be the first time that a governor had been thrown out of the Palácio das Princesas. Not so many years before, revolutionaries had chased another governor:

"He was a sugar-mill owner and loved parties and grand life. He escaped in a rush through the back of the palace, leaving in a boat dressed like a woman and wearing a wig."

"But our misfortune was that they put another sugar-mill owner in place of the sneak, and things remained just the same as before. But now the right man shall be placed in power," said Zé Luis, warming up to the debate.

But João Paulo's mother was pessimistic:

"It's no use, this won't change anything. Once on top, they all become dirty rats, and it's hard to remove these rats who hold on with all their might to the branches of power. The fight will be difficult. We need time and the patience of saints."

In front of Zé Luis' hovel a group of residents was ready to go to town braving the barrage to find out what really was going on. Before they could make up their minds, the firing started to diminish in intensity and became irregular and sporadic, until it finally stopped completely. A heavy silence hung over the landscape of the marshes. As night approached and João Paulo was still absent, his mother started to worry, saying:

"Where could João Paulo be in the midst of all this confusion? It's time for him to be home!"

Zé Luis answered, calming her:

"He must be at the priest's."

But the mother became more and more anxious and said she preferred to go and see if he was really there so she could be at peace. The whole group volunteered to go and search for João Paulo, thereby calming his worried mother.

They departed in the direction of the priest's house. The men went ahead, while the women followed with their frightened children clutching at their skirts. Maria asked everyone on the road if he had seen João Paulo. One little old woman had seen the boy and said she knew him quite well. This morning, she said, he had passed, running madly in the middle of the street. The woman had even warned him not to go toward the fighting, but he had paid no attention to her calls. He had kept running. . . .

The group arrived at the house of the priest; it was crowded with people who wanted news. The mother asked for João Paulo, and the priest informed her that the boy had not shown up that day. He had thought the boy was home with his parents. Fear grew in Maria's heart. She started to cry. The group decided to search the neighborhood in the company of Father Aristides. The latter marched ahead, the others respectfully keeping one step behind. Only the boy's mother moved impatiently ahead of the priest once in a while. Father Aristides tried to calm her, explaining what he thought had happened:

"Calm down, my child," he said. "You will soon find your son. He must be around, lost in the confusion. That's because this boy has always lived in intimate contact with the crabs, and his still unmolded child's soul must have taken the shape of a crab's soul, and today, when João Paulo heard the storm, he must have gone out of his mind, just like the crabs when they hear thunder. But the storm is over. Calm down, woman! Calm down, and you will soon find your son."

In their frantic search for João Paulo, the group encountered men covered with dust and with rifles in their hands. They spoke of the failure of the revolution:

"We were betrayed! We were beaten!" And distressed, they continued their march and disappeared in the shadows of the mangroves.

The greengrocer next to the bridge of Afogados informed the priest that that morning he had seen a boy running toward the bridge. The group moved in that direction. The greengrocer joined the group and showed where the heaviest fighting took place, all of which he had seen from the back window of his house.

They descended the slopes of the river and watched with anxious eyes as the high tide covered the mire and the mangroves of the river banks. The greengrocer explained:

"The rebels shot from this side, from these mangroves now covered by the water. The soldiers were divided into two groups. They shot in the direction of the bridge and from behind the mangroves on the other bank of the river. From home, I saw two in yellow uniforms, bending their wrists over the bushes, and then fall into the mire. Right there. . . ." And the man pointed at the immensity of the waters. It was as if he spoke of abstract things because nothing could be seen; only the high tide, roaring against the pillars of the bridge and licking the banks of the river. If underneath there were dead bodies from this morning's battle—and the man assured them there were—they would now be covered by this mass of water. How to find the little body of João Paulo in all this water?

"My God, what can we do?" asked the boy's mother.

"Let's start a search under the water," answered the greengrocer.

"But where? How?" asked Maria with dry lips and eyes steady on the current of the tide.

"Here, around the place where the battle took place," trustingly declared Father Aristides.

Chico, who had brought along the pole of his raft, started to explore the river bottom and entered the water till it reached his knees. The pole either got bogged down in the mud or stumbled over mangroves. Whenever it was stopped by something, there was a halt, followed by a questioning look on the faces of the people in the group. Chico explained:

"It is hard, it must be a mangrove root. Now, it is surely a stone. I hear the clang." And Chico struck the bottom of the river with the end of his pole.

As the search with the pole brought no results, it was suggested that they search for the body with a candle, a lighted candle that is put to float over the waters. It was Maria das Dores who suggested the idea.

"The lighted candle is placed in a gourd or in an empty can and is put to drift in the river along with our trust in God. The candle goes in search of the body and stops right on top of where the dead body lies."

The idea excited the group, although Father Aristides smacked his lips in disbelief. But he did not oppose it. And so the idea was put into action.

The light of the sun slowly disappeared in the sky as

186

the small flames started to float over the shining surface of water. There were lighted candles in gourds and paper boats made with old newspapers furnished by the greengrocer. Half a dozen of these strange boats drifted down the river. Two immediately floated away from the bank and were dragged by the current. They were totally indifferent to their mission. The others remained close to the edge and moved ahead slowly toward the sea. It was the hour of the ebb tide. The gourd placed in the water by Maria das Dores, who had an immovable faith in it, described two strange circles over the water and halted suddenly. Das Dores excitedly cried to the group:

"He must be here! Search over here!"

Chico used his pole. The spot was deep and the pole almost disappeared entirely in the water, but its tip hit something soft and strangely resistant. Chico trembled. Zé Luis tore his shirt off his back and plunged into the river. From the waters he dragged to the bank the heavy body of a man. His chest was pierced by bullets, his face swollen, his lips eaten away by *sirís,* and he showed his teeth, as if grinning at death.

The discovery reinforced the group's trust in the miraculous action of the candle. They continued to accompany the little boats that drifted downstream. Suddenly a strong gust of wind turned two of them over, drowning the candles in the darkness of the water. The remaining boats reached the pillars of the bridge and left indifferently, without transmitting any precise sign.

The mystery remained. Where could the poor boy be? The anguish grew. There was nothing to be done, so Father Aristides said decisively:

"We must return home to rest from the anxieties of this terrible day. You must get some sleep. Tomorrow, when the tide has receded and the sun has come out, we shall see what has happened. Patience, children, let God's will be done."

There was no opposition to his proposal. The group prepared to leave. Only Maria remained motionless, gazing in silence over the dark waters. Zé Luis pulled her gently toward home. They climbed the slope of the river and the group started to disperse.

Soon the news of João Paulo's disappearance spread throughout the neighborhood and caused as much effect as the failure of the revolution. The neighbors came to visit Zé Luis' family and spent the whole night at this strange wake. This was a wake for the absent body of João Paulo, which all knew to be far away at this hour in the mysterious kingdom of death. They spoke little, so as not to offend the pain of the parents. As they arrived, they almost spoke only through gestures: expressions on their faces revealing pain, gestures of resignation with their hands.

"That's how it is. . . ." And they lifted their hands, letting them fall again helplessly to their sides. Maria cried softly. Zé Luis said nothing.

Early next morning they departed again in search of the boy. The tide was low now, and they found huge patches of black mud and the ragged foliage of man-groves. They started the search again, getting stuck in the mire, and looked for the dead body as one looks for crabs. When the sun rose, a team of guards appeared. They were charged with the search for bodies. Several bodies of rebels and soldiers who had died in battle were found on either bank of the river. Some were removed from the mire already half eaten by the crabs and *siris*. Many had clenched fists and hardened fingers clinging tightly to the stocks of their rifles.

The search lasted all day. Regular shifts replaced each other, but João Paulo's body was nowhere to be found. Maria and Zé Luis did not leave the marshes and sought anxiously until almost the end of the day. Although exhausted, they gave up only when the waters of the tide mounted again, drowning everything—mangroves, mud, and their last hopes of finding their son's body. Their companions convinced them to go home. A funeral procession was formed and it crossed the marshes accompanying, instead of the body, the pain of the dead boy's parents. The people followed them to their hovel.

The sun was going down as the procession reached Stubborn Hamlet. The last rays of sunshine seemed to engrave with a firebrand on everyone's face the profound pain that overwhelmed them. Zé Luis, his eyes red, his lips dry, walked searching his tormented mind for the mysterious paths by which his son was led to death. Could it have been the pleasure he took in creating storms with Father Aristides? Or perhaps the bad example given by the *guaiamus* who lost their heads whenever they heard storms? Or was it, perhaps, the storm of ideas that Cosme had awakened in the boy's mind?

No one could help Zé Luis unfold this sad mystery. Little by little the night descended over the marsh and erased from Zé Luis' face the look of stone that all day long had made him seem like an outlaw.

And the landscape of the marshes was now covered by a veil of darkness, a black shroud that extended over all the bodies of the defeated revolutionists. Somewhere among them, buried under the mangroves, lay the body of João Paulo, whose flesh in decay would nourish the mud, which, in turn, feeds the cycle of the crab.